MW00804613

WILD GOOSE CHASE

WILD GOOSE CHASE

•

Mike Gaherty

AVALON BOOKS
NEW YORK

PRINTED IN THE UNITED STATES OF AMERICA
ON ACID-FREE PAPER
BY HADDON CRAFTSMEN, BLOOMSBURG, PENNSYLVANIA

For my brother

Chapter One

Ellie Regan sorted slowly through the layers of clothes piled several inches over the top of her suitcase, checking off what was there against a mental inventory. Finally satisfied, she pulled the soft lid down, leaned on it hard with one hand, and carefully worked the zipper around from one corner to the other. She stood the swollen piece of luggage on its edge on the bed and tried lifting it. She giggled out loud at the weight, more like a load of bricks than the clothes for a ten-day trip, she decided, but she did manage to wrestle the thing off the bed and stand it next to its smaller mate also packed to the limit.

"Are you about done in there?" It was her roommate, Erin Coglin, shouting from the living room of the comfortable apartment they shared. They were meeting some fellow teachers for dinner to celebrate the end of the school year, and they would be late if they didn't leave in the next few minutes.

"Be right there," Ellie called, then stopped for a quick look at herself in the full-length mirror on the back of the door. She combed her fingers through her dark hair, about all the attention the new, short summer cut required. She smiled at the colorful design on her T-shirt—a pink, fat satisfied bunny sitting on top of a pile of bright orange carrots. The lettering above his head was reversed in the mirror, but she knew what the words said—HELLO SUMMER. She knew because she'd done the tedious needlepoint herself during the whole oppres-

1

sive month of February just past—a February that had easily surpassed every other February in the Dubuque, Iowa, record book for snowfall. She smoothed the wraparound skirt that hugged her slim waist, wrinkled her nose at her image in the mirror, and stuck her tongue out at herself before hurrying out of the room.

The restaurant the five friends had chosen for their celebration was an expensive one perched high on a bluff overlooking the Mississippi River that stretched like a snake sunning itself as far as the eye could see both north and south. The young women settled noisily at the table set close to a broad window that provided an eagle's view of the river below and the bluffs to the east. They craned their necks to see the small boats flash up and down the river and one barge, black against the silvery river, moving so slowly against the current it seemed almost to be standing still.

The five were in high spirits at the prospect of a long summer's relief from the pressures of school. They had known each other for seven years now; they had met as freshmen at a small college on the opposite side of the state. The other four had tagged along when one, Alice Mason, drove to Dubuque for a job interview, and before they knew it, each had taken a job, two in high school and three in elementary. That was three years ago. Since then, two of the friends, Jan Peters and Nikki Frieze, had married. In fact, Jan was expecting a baby in August and wouldn't be teaching in the fall. Ellie's roommate, Erin, was planning her wedding for October. Ellie had already been picked to be the maid of honor.

The young women grew quiet as a starched waiter handed each a menu. Jan tried to balance the huge leather volume on her inflated midsection and caught Ellie's grin across the table. ''What are you laughing at? Your time will come. Say, when are you leaving, anyway?''

''Tomorrow morning—early.''

''All by yourself?'' asked Nikki with a disapproving frown.

''Sure, unless I can talk Erin into going.'' She looked at

her roommate with a raised eyebrow. "She doesn't have a thing to do but sit around the pool all day."

"I told you Jerry would have a fit if I left right now with all the wedding plans still up in the air."

"Give me a break. You're not getting married for practically five months. It would only be for ten days. You ought to be able to tear yourselves away from each other for that long. Anyway, you're going to be looking at each other every day for the next fifty years."

"Don't make it sound like such torture."

"Hey, you two, settle down," Jan commanded. "Just wait till love hits you between the eyes, Miss Regan. Then you'll understand. And speaking of love, how are things between you and the good Dr. Evans?"

Ellie screwed her face up into a look that would stop a barge on the river below them, and her roommate explained for her. "We don't mention the E word anymore. The bad Dr. Evans, formerly the good Dr. Evans, has fallen out of favor with the picky Miss Regan."

"Whoops," Jan said. "Sorry I brought it up. So what was wrong with him? I always thought he was kind of cute."

Ellie waved a hand of dismissal. "It's no big deal. He's very nice. I guess I just knew quite a while ago he wasn't the one." She pushed out her lower lip into an exaggerated pout. "Maybe I'll just end up an old maid."

Erin nodded her head with certainty. "I'm telling you, she's too picky. She can find something wrong with any man."

"That's not true," Ellie insisted. "I just like to have a man pay as much attention to me as he does to his latest stupid research project."

Alice put an arm around her. "Oh, poor, poor Ellie. Is it time for the blind date?"

Ellie pulled away in exaggerated horror. "Oh, no, please, anything but the blind date."

"I never did like the way that Dr. Evans cut his hair, anyway," observed Nikki as if she were in a world of her own. "He always looked like one of the Three Stooges. I don't know which one. I think it was Moe."

The other four laughed. ''At least you know you have Nikki's approval for the breakup,'' said Jan. ''By the way,'' she added in an obvious attempt to change the subject, ''what's this I hear about a wild goose chase after an oil well?''

Ellie straightened in her chair. ''Who told you about that?'' Jan pointed a finger at Erin, and Ellie glared at her roommate. ''What's the idea of calling it a wild goose chase, anyway?''

Erin held her hands out in a gesture of innocence. ''Don't look at me. The words 'wild goose chase' never passed my lips.''

The others closed their menus to give undivided attention to such exciting news. ''What's this all about?'' Alice asked.

''Yeah, what gives?'' Nikki chimed in.

''It's no big deal,'' Ellie said.

''Go ahead, tell 'em,'' her roommate broke in. ''Ellie's going to be rolling in money.''

''Oh, stop it. You're just making fun.''

''No, I'm not. I think it sounds exciting.''

Jan raised her menu in a threatening gesture. ''So, are you going to tell us or do we have to beat it out of you?'' They all laughed.

Ellie looked over the group. ''Okay, you asked for it.'' She took a deep breath and began her story. ''Last summer when my dad died, my mom and I were going through the safety deposit box and we found an oil stock that my grandfather bought in 1939. It was issued by the LeClaire Oil Syndicate in the amount of one thousand dollars.''

''You're kidding,'' Nikki broke in. ''And that's the first you knew of it?''

''Well, no, not exactly. I knew about it, but I'd never seen it. My dad used to joke about it all the time. Whenever my mom wanted to buy something, he'd always say we couldn't afford it until Grandpa's oil well came in.'' Their waiter suddenly appeared, and Ellie had to delay her story while they each ordered.

As the waiter headed toward the kitchen loaded down with

their menus, the four women all eyed Ellie eagerly. "Well?" Jan asked. "So you found out you own an oil well?"

"Don't I wish," Ellie said with a grin. "I highly doubt it. But the place where the stock or share or whatever you call it was issued was in Wyoming. Elkhorn County to be exact, which is on the east side of the state. It's right on the edge of the Black Hills in South Dakota, and I've always wanted to go there so I decided I'd see Mount Rushmore and the Badlands and all that other touristy stuff first and then slip over into Wyoming and check out my oil well." She laughed at the thought. "Kill two birds with one stone, as my dad used to say."

Alice had a perplexed look on her face. "1939 is a long time ago. Didn't your grandfather ever hear anything about it in all those years?"

"Not a word. It sounds strange, but he was sure he'd been swindled about ten minutes after he paid his money. Ten minutes too late. He was a farmer in Iowa. My grandpa, that is. According to what my dad told us, some guy drove into the farmyard one December day selling this surefire deal in an oil well, and my grandpa bit on it to the tune of a thousand dollars, which was a lot of money then, especially during the Depression."

"It's *still* a lot of money," Jan said with a shake of the head.

"Right," Ellie agreed, "but you wouldn't consider it your life savings now, which I guess my grandpa did. So he never heard anything more, and finally after two years or so, he wrote a letter to the man whose name appeared on the stock. He didn't even know where to send it because there wasn't a town or city listed on the stock—just Elkhorn County, Wyoming, so that's where he sent it. And it came back with a note that it couldn't be delivered without a complete address."

"Sounds like your grandpa got taken big time," Nikki said.

"I suppose so. About that time World War Two came along, and my grandpa had to go. When he got back after the war, the certificate must have been buried in a drawer somewhere and he just forgot about it. Or tried to forget about it.

Dad always said they were ashamed of it. Grandpa and Grandma, I mean. I guess they felt like they were pretty stupid for giving so much money to some total stranger. Anyway, they never mentioned it again. At least as far as my dad could remember. They didn't want anyone to know what they'd done, he always guessed. He found it when Grandpa died.''

"Were your grandparents alive when you were little?'' Alice asked.

"Oh, sure. I used to stay with them on the farm for two or three weeks every summer. And we used to have fun Christmases at their place.'' Her face clouded. "But they died when I was twelve years old. In the same year. Grandpa died first of cancer, and Grandma just gave up after that. She didn't live six months.''

The group fell silent. "That happens a lot,'' Jan observed finally. "So you really are on a wild goose chase. It sounds exciting, though,'' she added quickly.

"Have you ever thought of hiring an investigator to search out the thing?'' Nikki asked. "Paul has a cousin who was adopted, and she had someone find her brother who'd been adopted by another family.''

Ellie nodded. "I know I've thought of that, but I hate to spend money for something that probably isn't worth the paper it's printed on. I mean the chance that anything could ever come of it is pretty remote. I bet the odds are even worse than winning the lottery. The guy probably just made off with the money. For all anyone knows he might not have even been from Wyoming.''

"Does the certificate look all official and everything?'' Jan asked.

"Sure.'' Ellie reached for her purse which was dangling from the back of her chair by its strap. "I've got it with me.''

"You carry it around with you?'' Alice wanted to know.

"Well, not all the time, but I'm bringing it along on my wild goose chase.'' She emphasized the last three words for effect. As a matter of fact she was beginning to think those words made a pretty good description of the trip she was about to make. She knew the whole thing was silly, but it was exciting. She slipped the paper out of her purse and held it up. It was smaller than they had all been expecting. Only a little larger than a check out of a checkbook. The four leaned closer, definitely caught up in the excitement that the small piece of paper was generating. It certainly was very official looking, done on light-brown document paper with the hint of a design running through its background. There was even a dark decorative border, the kind you might expect to see on something very important and legal. And after sixty years it had just the right look of age, wrinkled from being folded and frayed slightly around the edges.

"Oh, let me see," Nikki begged. Ellie handed it over. Nikki examined the piece of paper carefully, barely able to control her excitement. She saw the dark penstroke naming Ellie's grandfather, Peter J. Regan, as the owner of one thousand profit-sharing units in the J. P. LeClaire Oil Syndicate. The bold, dark signature at the bottom was that of none other than Jerome P. LeClaire himself, and he was identified as the sole trustee in tiny lettering under his name. "They must have thought they were dealing with the CEO himself," she said, pointing at the name.

"I suppose," Ellie agreed, "but how many CEOs go wandering around the countryside selling shares in their companies?"

The certificate made its way slowly around the table. Alice looked up from her study of it. "What about other people in the neighborhood? Weren't there others who bought one of these?"

Ellie nodded. "I thought about that, too. All I can figure is they were all so ashamed they didn't want to tell anyone else they'd been scammed. And another thing you've got to remember, this was in the country where your nearest neighbors might be miles away, and you wouldn't see them very often."

Jan had been putting her analytical mind to the topic. She suddenly brightened. "I know what I'd do if I were going to pull a scam like that. I'd just drive cross-country and stop at places miles and miles apart. That way nobody could organize to call the law or anything."

"Why, Jan, what a devious mind," Erin said with a grin.

"No, I mean it, it's a perfect plan. Almost a divide-and-conquer scheme. It wouldn't work today, though. Communication is too good. Someone would call a reporter, and the next thing you know it'd be on the national news."

Erin's grin turned to a laugh. "Don't sound so disappointed."

Alice was staring at the stained-glass lamp hanging over their table, deep in thought. She hadn't even heard what Jan had said. "How are you going to go about this?" she asked. "I mean, are you just going to go into this county . . . what'd you said it was?"

"Elkhorn County."

"Right, this Elkhorn County and start asking every person you see if they know someone by the name of . . ." She craned her neck to see the name on the certificate which Nikki was studying again. ". . . LeClaire?"

"Well, actually I've kind of already done that."

Nikki looked up. "What do you mean?"

"I used the computer. That national telephone directory on the Net. I looked up LeClaire in both the yellow pages and the white pages. And I didn't find any listings in Wyoming."

Alice raised an eyebrow. "Hmm. That complicates things. So that means he never existed. By that name, I mean. Or he died without leaving any family."

"Or he made a pot of money and moved to Paris," Erin suggested. They all laughed.

"If he's still alive, he'd be ancient, wouldn't he?" asked Jan.

Ellie nodded. "I suppose he'd have to be in his mideighties—at least."

Jan persisted. "So what *is* your plan?" She never liked to start anything without some kind of plan.

Ellie smiled. "You're the one who should be coming with me. You'd have everything worked out before we got there."

Jan patted her stomach. "You're forgetting I've got a prior commitment this summer."

"I know." Ellie took a deep breath and worked in a shrug

at the same time. "To answer your question, I guess I don't have much of a plan. I thought I'd go to Burnbridge first. That's the county seat. I thought I'd nose around the courthouse and see if I can find anything official about a claim or drilling rights or whatever they have to have to drill for oil. And maybe if they have a retirement home I'll go there and ask some of the folks if they ever knew a Jerome LeClaire." That last idea just came to her out of the blue that very moment, and she was rather proud of it.

Jan was less than impressed. "That's your plan? To visit an Alzheimer's ward to see if anyone remembers somebody who might have lived there sixty years ago?"

Ellie's defense came from where she least expected it— Nikki. "Just 'cause a person's in their eighties doesn't mean they have Alzheimer's," the young woman said with just a touch of anger in her voice. "My grandpa's eighty-six, and he's still just as sharp mentally as about anyone I know."

"I know that, Nikki," Jan said. "I was exaggerating. But you have to admit that's not much of a plan."

Ellie shook her head. "You and your plans. Don't you think you're taking this a little too seriously? Remember, you're the one who called it a wild goose chase. I'm going on vacation. Could it cause any harm to look around a little bit while I'm in the neighborhood?"

"For oil wells," Nikki added. "Don't forget that. For oil wells."

"Right," Ellie said. She tried to keep a smile off her face as she added, "I've been studying Wyoming. If I have to talk to everyone in the state to find out what I want, it won't be all that hard. There are only two people per square mile in the whole state."

"You're kidding!" Alice said.

"Nope. Two people per square mile. It'll be a piece of cake."

"Are you going to walk each of those square miles or ride a horse?" Jan asked with a grin.

"There you go with your plans again." Ellie pursed her

lips in thought. "I think I'll ride a horse. I've always liked horses."

"Well, we wish you luck," said Alice. "Don't we, girls?" They all nodded their agreement. "Just don't forget about your old, poor friends in Dubuque when you make your first million."

Ellie laughed as she slipped the stock certificate back into her purse. "Fat chance," she said.

"Please don't say fat," Jan pleaded as she patted her stomach, and the friends broke into laughter. Just then the waiter arrived with their salads.

Chapter Two

Ellie didn't get away as early the next morning as she'd hoped. She was up at 6:00 as planned and dressed in less than half an hour. She rolled her two suitcases as quietly as she could to the front door and began fixing a light breakfast in the tiny kitchen. It was about that time Erin came dragging out, stretching and yawning, to see her roommate off, and the two dawdled over coffee talking about last night's dinner and plans for the summer and, of course, the wedding. It wasn't until well after 7:30 that Ellie backed her Toyota away from the curb and waved to her roommate standing near the front door in her robe and slippers. Ellie hadn't really given up on talking Erin into making the trip until last night. And it wouldn't have been entirely out of the question to see her come out with her suitcase packed in the morning, ready to go. Erin was famous for doing things spur of the moment. But not this time.

Ellie headed north out of the city, the highway angling slightly west as it followed the river. She could see the river off to her right, impressive but nothing compared to what it would become downstream. She had seen it near St. Louis where it joined forces with the Missouri and knew that was still a mere trickle to what it would become before flowing into the Gulf. Less than five miles outside the city the highway took a turn to the left, leaving the river and heading directly west.

Ellie knew this highway, had traveled it often with her parents though not for years. She grew up in Bloomington, Illinois, but went with her mom and dad often enough to visit her grandparents on their farm near Walnut Grove just this side of Mason City. She always remembered Dubuque as definitely more than halfway on those never-ending odysseys to the farm, and she guessed she probably became a particularly obnoxious backseat traveler at about that point. But it was always so hard to sit still when they were going to the farm.

She hadn't traveled this way for so long, nearly everything seemed strange and new to her, but there were odd moments of déjà vu. Like when the highway passed through a tiny town, Forest Bluff it was, and dipped beneath a railroad underpass. The concrete supports on both sides were painted with colorful graffiti, mostly high school graduation years and the initials proclaiming young love. The years and the initials had changed, but she suddenly felt an overpowering sense of recollection. She was in the backseat again. *"When are we going to get there?"* she could almost hear herself asking.

Then there was the big red barn with the Mail Pouch Tobacco sign painted on its side. She always knew when she saw that barn, they were only minutes from the farm. Fifteen years ago that sign was faded almost beyond reading. Now it was little more than a discoloration on the gray weathered siding of a barn that was listing precariously toward the west. Ellie wondered if she would remember where to turn off the hard-surface road. Then she saw it—the bridge with its half-moon steel sides that seemed to tower over her when she came here with her grandpa to kick stones into the placid stream below. Now, as she passed over it, the bridge seemed puny compared with her memory of it.

She turned right at the next corner and continued along a gravel road up a gentle rise with neat rows of fresh green corn plants stretching away from the road on both sides. And suddenly there it was, almost hidden by a cluster of untended trees—the house that would forever live in her memory as a place of such love and happiness. To her surprise the house was all that remained of the once-neat homestead. The barn and other outbuildings were gone and in their place the en-croaching field of young corn reaching almost to the fence surrounding the house and yard. In that first split-second of recognition, the thought struck her that she never should have made this side trip. As she drew nearer and caught sight of the thigh-high grass choking her grandmother's prized flower beds, the broken windows, the peeled and faded paint, the length of gutter dangling from the eaves, the thought hardened to a certainty. This house, the overgrown yard, the apple trees with their tangle of broken limbs—all of it would have been better left to the gentle treatment of her memory.

She slowed at the driveway, used now only by tractors pull-ing pieces of heavy equipment. She didn't turn in but came to a stop directly in front of the house. As she stared out the open window at the scene in front of her, working hard to spot the links to the past rather than the obvious signs of ruin, an odd thing happened. She remembered her wild goose chase. Nearly sixty years ago, she thought, *he* drove up that very lane, this Jerome LeClaire. She suddenly felt such a curious anger at the old injury to her grandfather's pride, to say noth-ing of his Depression bank account, that her jaw clenched and she gripped the steering wheel hard. The curiousness of her anger struck even her. After all, the grievance was generations old. But her brain was working overtime to give flesh and blood to this stranger from the past. She could almost see the sly smile as he pocketed the wad of bills and climbed into his car on the way to his next unsuspecting investor.

She forced her thoughts in other directions to try to push such ideas out of her head. She remembered the official-looking document tucked in her purse and her dad's gentle joking about its assumed worthlessness. But suddenly she couldn't feel the humor in the thing at all. It was because of her grandfather, Peter J. Regan himself, that she couldn't. She'd never heard him joke about it. Never even heard him mention it so far as she could remember. As she sat there in front of his decaying homestead, her foot pressed against the brake pedal, she pictured him again as she would always re-member him, bibbed overalls stretched tight over an expanse of midsection, white hair looking windblown even when he was sitting serenely in his straight-back chair at the head of the table, face and neck and arms perpetually browned from his exposure to the sun.

And his smile, always the smile, especially for her. Even when she got into trouble, by her carelessness or just because she didn't know any better. Like one time she'd never forget. She couldn't have been more than seven or eight. She was exploring, as usual, when she spotted a big bunch of cows staring at her across a fence, looking sad-faced and curious all at the same time. Without a thought, she unlatched the big farm gate and swung it open to let them out. She could re- member the sinking feeling in her stomach when the thought struck her that she'd done something really bad this time. The black-and-white bodies bolted past her, heading for the lane and then the road like they'd been planning for a long time where to go if such an opportunity ever presented itself.

She could remember as if it were yesterday her tearful ex- planation after she saw the mess she'd caused. She felt sorry for them, she'd whimpered. They looked like they wanted to do some exploring. Grandpa was mopping his brow with a big red handkerchief as he listened to her story. She just knew she'd made him mad this time. He'd spent the better part of an hour trying to coax the cows back through the gate into the field where they belonged. But her fear was short-lived as she saw the smile spread across his face. He hugged her to his side. ''There, there, now, that's all right. No harm done. I expect you just might be right. Those girls were so happy goin' exploring they acted like they never wanted to come home.''

She knew he was the kind of man whose word was his bond and who expected the same in those he dealt with. She remembered her dad's account of the time Grandpa sold ten cows to a neighbor. Two weeks later one of the cows dropped dead in the field. Grandpa heard about it while attending a farm sale. He searched through the crowd for the neighbor who had no thought of pressing a claim for the dead cow, which could have died for any number of reasons. But

Grandpa insisted, so the story went, pulled out his billfold, and refunded the man's money. No wonder he was an easy target for Mr. Jerome LeClaire, Ellie decided. He assumed that same honesty in everyone else. A steady roar in the distance brought her eyes to the rearview mirror. A tractor was bearing down on her from behind. She let her foot slip from the brake pedal, gave a last look toward the house, and sped off down the road.

She turned left at the next corner, drove on deep in thought for another mile, and turned left again. She knew this road would return her to the hard-surfaced one she had left earlier. But before she reached the stop sign, she'd made up her mind. She would leave the sight-seeing for the return trip. Instead she would head straight for Burnbridge. She would do what her grandfather hadn't done over sixty years ago. She would find out just what did happen to this Jerome LeClaire after he drove out of the Regan farmstead. The thought of a stored-up treasure, which had lurked tantalizingly in the back of her brain, was all but gone. She well knew the chances of finding even a trace of some oil conglomerate that her grandfather might have a part interest in was rarer than finding a valuable penny in the coffee can on her closet shelf where she tossed her loose change. But who could tell? If someone or some group profited from her grandfather's money, she would press a claim. If for no other reason than to set matters right with his memory.

She squinted into the distance for any oncoming cars and eased her Toyota back onto the blacktop road. Could he still be alive? she wondered. He'd be pretty old. It had been sixty years. No one ever mentioned how old Jerome LeClaire was, she remembered. But then no one really saw him but Grandpa and Grandma, and they never talked about it. Assuming he was in his mid-twenties, he'd be well into his eighties by now. It was possible. But not very. His name wasn't in the Wyoming telephone directory when she checked it on the computer. So, if he was alive, he must not still be living *there*. As a new thought struck her, she pursed her lips, revealing a thin frown line that appeared from just above the bridge of her nose onto the otherwise smooth skin of her forehead. *Why didn't I run his name through the other state directories? It would have taken all of fifteen minutes. Now, I may be going all this way for nothing.*

She drove on toward Walnut Grove wondering if she would remember the tiny town where her grandpa and grandma had done their shopping and banking and socializing. She remembered going with them to church there when she visited, and she was pleased to spot the tall brick steeple off to her right as she drove toward the town square. The town still had a familiar feel to it, and she was glad about that. She remembered the square with its park and bandshell where they—her mom and dad and grandpa and grandma—all went to a concert one July Fourth. She parked, took her maps with her, and walked an entire circuit of the square satisfied that the stores still looked reasonably prosperous.

She slipped into a tidy coffee shop, ordered a cup of coffee and a sinful pecan roll (she was on vacation, she reminded herself), and spread out the maps in front of her. So much for a leisurely trip through Iowa and South Dakota, she decided. She'd do her meandering, looking at the sights, shopping for antiques, the fun stuff on the return trip. She traced with her forefinger a faster route, all interstate, to Wyoming. She would catch I-35 just west of Mason City. If she took that north just barely into Minnesota, she could meet up with I-90 and go straight through South Dakota into Wyoming. The interstate wasn't the best way to see the countryside, she knew from experience, but it would have to do until she got this oil business taken care of. She took a sip of coffee and broke off another portion of her enormous pecan roll. It really was becoming a wild goose chase, she decided, remembering her friend Jan's words to describe the trip.

That night she stayed in Mitchell, South Dakota. She was exhausted after watching mile markers slip past all day and fell into bed after a quick shower. She had eaten her dinner, such as it was, at a fast-food restaurant outside Sioux Falls. When she finally closed her eyes, she could still see the double ribbon of white highway stretching away ahead of her. But not for long. If she replayed in her dreams her day behind the wheel, she remembered none of it the next morning. She slept better than she had in months and awoke refreshed, ready to do it all over again. On this second day she traveled through miles of farmland, the fields of corn and beans and wheat soaking up artificial rain spouting in gentle arcs from mazes of tubing on wheels that were tracing giant circles through the fields.

Near Chamberlain she stopped at an overlook, got out of her car, and gazed down at a valley stretching as far as she could see to the north and the fast-moving river, the Missouri, that had carved that valley. Even from this distance she could see the roiled brown of the water that had earned the river its nickname, the Muddy Mo. Seeing the river from this vantage point reminded her of her friends back home and their end-of-the-year dinner. She doubted they would approve of her change in plan, her crazy rush to get to Wyoming. She smiled. Maybe Nikki would. She seemed more excited than the others at the prospect of finding an oil well. But not Jan. Definitely not Jan. She never liked doing things spur-of-the-moment.

Ellie knew she would be hard-pressed to explain to her friends what had happened yesterday as she looked at the old farmhouse. She wasn't sure herself. She guessed she felt closer to her grandparents as she sat there looking at their house. That was it probably. She felt tuned in to their feelings more than she had for years, maybe more than she ever had since now she could look back on their lives with a degree of maturity of her own. It was hard not to feel sorry for a man who had made a bad business investment at a time when money must have been so hard to come by. A thought struck her. Where did he come up with that much money? Her dad had never really talked about it, but that must have been every penny they possessed in the world. She studied the river in the distance. *It's amazing they didn't lose the farm over that. I'll bet there were some sleepless nights in that old house. But he still managed to do well for himself and his family.* She had to wonder what his dreams were—if he still hoped a letter one day would inform him of the fabulous success of that earlier wild venture. Thinking about those imagined false hopes made her angry all over again.

And she had to admit seeing the farm the way it had become hadn't done anything for her frame of mind either. But why? she asked herself, trying to be logical. Everything changed. The farm was out of the family. It was sold years ago because no one was left to take it over. The new farmer obviously had no interest in living in the house. Eventually he'd tear it down, she guessed. That would be better anyway. She preferred the memory of the old place with all the perfection that memory has to offer rather than the reality she knew existed now. But why was she taking things out on Jerome LeClaire? He was just a run-of-the-mill scam artist who probably died years ago. Then her overactive imagination conjured up once again the slippery, oily image that had become Jerome LeClaire to her, and she climbed back into the Toyota ready to follow his trail wherever it led.

The land changed gradually as she continued west. The lush green of irrigated fields gave way to stunted, yellowed rows of corn and beans and patchy fields of wheat struggling to survive in the thin layer of topsoil that rested uncomfortably on a bed of rock and sand. She saw expanses of grass extending on both sides of the road as far as she could see. Spinning windmills dotted the valleys between the low hills pumping water into round tanks that attracted crowds of thirsty cows of all sizes and colors. She pulled in for lunch at a busy restaurant near the highway. A sign advertising buffalo burgers some miles back had caught her attention, and once seated in the noisy dining room, she ordered one, imagining what Nikki's reaction would be when she told her. It was always fun to shock Nikki. Her friends seemed to try to outdo each other at it, and Ellie was convinced Nikki exaggerated her reaction just a little because she enjoyed the attention.

Ellie looked about her. She saw the usual groups of tourists in their shorts and bright tops and white tennies on their way to the Black Hills. But she spotted the locals, too. They were a weather-hardened lot in their own kind of uniform—worn jeans, faded blue denim shirts, leather boots, and, of course, cowboy hats, sweat-stained and securely in place on their heads even at the table. Ellie took it all in as she munched on her burger, which was very good—a little drier than a regular hamburger but full of flavor all the same. She made a mental note of the taste for Nikki's benefit and took a long look around the dining room imagining how she would liven her buffalo burger story with a little local color.

She pushed on, the sameness of the countryside making her so drowsy at one point she pulled into a rest stop and dozed for fifteen minutes sitting upright in her seat. As she drove on, she became aware of more changes in the land. The gentle hills were giving way to a rougher setting. Exposed jumbles of rock and gashes cutting into the hills hinted at the Badlands that lay ahead. Ellie had seen the billboards inviting a brief detour into the Badlands National Park, but she still intended to save that for the return trip. She saw, off in the distance on her left as she approached, the moonscape of those Badlands formed by the eroded and eroding sandstone. She definitely would stop there on the way back. And she was curious about the town of Wall, South Dakota, on her right. She would check that out, too. She had seen the famous Wall Drug signs for the past three hundred miles at least. What could be so attractive about a drugstore? she wondered as she watched many of the cars she'd been sharing the highway with, slow and take the exit.

As she drew closer to Rapid City, she became aware of the famous hills jutting into the horizon, dark and shadowed by the forests of fir and pine covering them from head to toe. She was pleased to see they really were black hills. She stayed with the interstate as it skirted the northern edge of the city nestled just to the east of the hills, again resisting the temptation to take the offramp designated as the shortest route to Mount Rushmore and its famous carving. Now the highway climbed into those hills and Ellie thought to herself she would be more than happy to call them full-fledged mountains if she'd never seen the Rockies. They were still impressive and so beautiful. She stopped at a pulloff just to jump out and smell the clear, pine-scented air. She passed the town of Dead-wood, made infamous by the shooting of Wild Bill Hickok. At Spearfish she left the interstate and took a highway heading south. The new highway cut through a forest of dense pine which thinned abruptly as she crossed the state line into Wyoming.

The countryside changed yet again, this time to a flat expanse of grassland stretching away to the distant horizon. A highway marker announced the distance to Burnbridge—twenty-four miles. A movement to her right caught Ellie's attention, and her pulse quickened as she glanced quickly in that direction. A lone oil pumper was working slowly, rhythmically, its headlike boom seeming to bow to the ground with each thrust of its pumprod into the well. She saw more of the pumpers as she continued. Not all of them were working but enough were to convince her that oil was still a vital part of this area. At least Jerome LeClaire wasn't lying when he said there was oil out here, she thought to herself with a grin. She passed what she guessed to be a refinery on the outskirts of the town. Just inside the city limits she saw a multistory office building adjacent to a cluster of tanks and barrels and shops and warehouses. A brick sign nestled in the middle of a fenced, well-manicured lawn in front of the office building proclaimed the complex the Lassiter Petroleum Company.

Ellie was feeling the effects of a second day of steady driving. It was 6:30 local time, but her stomach was still operating on the time back home, one hour later, and she was starved. She took a drive through the main street of the town to orient herself. She saw what she guessed was the county courthouse on her left. Its distinctive gray cupola attracted her first, and she slowed to look for a sign. There it was: The Elkhorn County Courthouse. She would start there in the morning. She found a comfortable motel adjacent to a lumber warehouse with great stacks of freshly cut lumber. She breathed deeply of the heavenly fresh pine smell as she got out of her car to go into the motel office. After she lugged her suitcases into the room and settled herself, she climbed reluctantly back into the car to search for a restaurant. She found one just off Main Street that was anything but fancy, but the food was good, and that's all she cared about just now. She took a stroll through the main part of downtown after dinner and noted that some of the stores were boarded up. She wondered if a small town like this could be experiencing flight to the suburbs just like the big cities. She made her way back to her motel, read a travel book she had bought at a gas station minimart in the afternoon until she couldn't keep her eyes open, and went to bed.

Chapter Three

Ellie crawled out of bed the next morning short on sleep from a night of tossing and turning but still anxious to get started. She knew she could use one of Jan's plans right now, but she would have to make do with her own ingenuity. She thought of her first move as she stood under the hot shower letting life slowly return to her body. She'd start first at the courthouse, ask a few questions, and see if anyone had ever heard of Mr. Jerome LeClaire. Not likely, she decided, considering how long ago all this had taken place. But she could try the deeds office to see if there was anything on file about the guy.

She let the delicious spray cascade over her neck and upper back to ease a stiffness she was feeling there either from the long hours of driving but more likely from the bag of sand that had been masquerading as her pillow all last night. She vowed never to leave home again without her own Mr. Fluff. She was beginning to feel almost human again as she toweled off slowly. She waved the hair dryer in the direction of her hair for less than a minute and then shaped it with some fluffs of her hand after she finally found herself in the fogged bathroom mirror. She grinned at the effect, deciding that if this summer cut became a year-round thing, she could sleep an extra fifteen minutes in the morning come next fall and the start of school. Next she changed into dark slacks and a white blouse, sat on the bed to slip on a pair of sandals, and thought about breakfast for the first time—especially a cup of strong black coffee. That would complete the waking-up process. She thought she remembered something about a complimentary continental breakfast, and she glanced through a colorful flyer on top of the television set to confirm her recollection. She would try it today to avoid having to search for another restaurant.

She was glad she did. The coffee was excellent, and the fresh long johns weren't bad either, but most important of all the information she picked up was useful. The breakfast was served in a tiny room with a large window looking out on the stacked fresh lumber in the lot across the street. There were three round, white, Formica tables with two straight-back, wooden chairs tucked under each. A counter, complete with sink, held the coffeemaker, a juice dispenser, and three cardboard boxes of pastry. Ellie was the only guest taking advantage of the free breakfast just now, and the day clerk left her place in the office, stuck her head in the door to see if everything was all right, and then lingered, leaning against the door frame to do just about her favorite thing—talk. Ellie tried to judge the woman's age but gave up. She decided she could be anywhere from fifty-five to eighty. That was her best guess. She had the drawn, deeply wrinkled face of a woman in her seventies or even older, but her gravel-like voice and persistent cough hinted that the wrinkles might be the result of a lifetime of cigarette smoking. Her hair, dyed an unusual reddish blond, was pulled into a tight bun at the back of her head. Her eyes, a faded brown, had an inquisitive look to them. She obviously liked people, Ellie decided, especially if she could learn their story.

"What brings a pretty thing like you into this wild country?" she began in her raspy voice.

Ellie studied the woman over her cup of coffee. "Oh, just traveling around, seeing the sights."

"Ain't much to see 'round here," she said with a short laugh that sounded more like a snort. "Dubuque? That's way on the other side of the state, as I recollect."

She'd been studying the check-in card, Ellie decided, or

maybe she'd seen her license plate. "Right. On the Mississippi River."

"You *are* a long way from home. Travel a lot, do ya?" She was fishing.

Ellie decided to trade a snippet of personal information in exchange for what this woman might be able to tell her about the oil business. "No, not really. I'm a high school teacher. Well, counselor really." She saw the woman's faint smile of satisfaction that her fishing had been successful. "The truth is I've always wanted to see the Black Hills and all the touristy things around there, and I decided I'd make a little side trip to Burnbridge. My grandpa bought into an oil well somewhere right around here a long time ago, and I decided to see whatever happened to it." She saw the woman's eyes brighten and knew she'd struck pay dirt.

"Hope you ain't countin' on gettin' rich," the woman said with a laugh that turned into a hacking cough requiring attention from a tissue tucked up the sleeve of her faded green sweatshirt. "You ain't the first and you probably won't be the last. *Lot of* wildcatters paid for their wells by sellin' shares. Trouble is, most of them wells turned out to be dry holes. My daddy was a worker in the fields back in the thirties when everbody had oil fever. He used to tell me, 'Lil, if I had a dollar for every worthless hole dug in this state, I'd be a rich man.' There's lots of dry holes sunk out there," she said as she waved a hand in the direction of the window. "Then, too, ya had some men just tryin' to get rich playin' on everbody else's ideas about gettin' rich. Ya always have that kind hangin' around. They collected the money but didn't dig no wells. My daddy used to tell about them, too."

Ellie was thinking about Jerome LeClaire. Was he one of those kind? She had a pretty good idea he probably was. "Is there any record of those old companies?"

"The ones on the up-and-up, sure. A few of 'em are still around. Most of 'em were bought up by bigger companies. But the oil business is way down around here. Not like it used to be. A lot of the fields are about petered out. They're havin' to use some of those tricks to get the last oil out. And sometimes it just ain't worth it to get the oil out. Not till the price goes up a lot more than now. What's the name of the company you're lookin' for?''

Ellie smiled at the thought that her search might end right here in the continental breakfast room of the Pine Rest Motel with a woman by the name of Lil. ''The name of the man who sold the stock to my grandfather was Jerome LeClaire. It was called the LeClaire Oil Syndicate.''

The woman knitted her brow in thought. ''LeClaire? No, I can't remember that name. Did he live around here?''

''I don't really know. All I know is no one by that name lives here now. But I suppose he would be long dead anyway. All this happened over sixty years ago.''

''No, I can't recall that name. If my daddy was still alive, he'd be able to tell us in a minute. He had his faculties sharp as ever up till the very day he died. Some of the folks at the Elk Creek Retirement Home go back that far. 'Course, some of 'em, bless 'em, don't know what day of the week it is. So, ya say your granddad bought oil stock off this LeClaire fellow?''

''Right. My grandfather was a farmer back in Iowa, and LeClaire stopped in one day selling shares in an oil syndicate located in Burnbridge.''

The woman nodded and snorted again knowingly. ''Oh, so that's the story. He might not even have been from here. Could have just picked this place 'cause it was a big oil town about then.''

Ellie finished off the rest of her coffee which had begun to cool during the conversation. ''I've thought of that.''

''Your best bet's the Howard Parker Museum.''

''The Howard Parker Museum?''

''Right. He was a banker in town a long time ago. Got shot and killed during a big bank robbery. His wife left money for a town museum, and it's a good one, too. Got lots of stuff about oil.''

Ellie nodded, thinking to herself. Her breakfast had definitely been profitable. She almost had a plan. Jan would be proud. ''Thanks. Thanks a lot. I'll try this museum.''

"Right," Lil said, happy that someone was taking her advice. "I got some literature about it in the office. I'll look it up. And you might wanta try Elk Creek, too." Her face brightened with a sudden idea. "Elmer Williams."

"Excuse me?" Ellie asked with a confused smile.

"Elmer Williams. He's your man. I should of thought of him right off. He's up at the Elk Creek Home. Ninety-five if he's a day. Friend of my daddy's. If anybody'd remember this fella that stiffed your grandpa, he would. Don't know how good his head's workin' nowadays, but most folks up there remember old stuff better'n what they had for breakfast. Yup, Elmer Williams might just know somethin'. Now, let's see—you're wantin' somethin' on the museum." She scurried off to look for the brochure, and Ellie stood to clear her table, amused, but at the same time impressed, at this woman's obvious willingness to help her guests.

She stuck with her plan to go to the courthouse first. She parked across the street from the impressive, gold-domed structure, darted across, and climbed the dozen or so worn steps to the heavy wooden door. She stepped inside to a musty smell and the forbidding look of dark, heavily varnished woodwork everywhere. She climbed a short flight of stairs to a broad hallway with a series of offices opening off of it. She turned slowly, reading the white lettering on the black signs suspended next to each door until she found what she was looking for—Register of Deeds. She went through the door and up to an ornate but worn wooden counter. Two young women were working at desks separated by a row of gray metal filing cabinets and a jumble of office equipment. The closer one stood up quickly and came to the counter. She was a slender redhead with an easy smile. "Can I help you?"

Ellie leaned on the counter. "Maybe, but it's kind of a long shot. I'm trying to find out if a man by the name of Jerome LeClaire ever owned property in this area. If he did, it would have been a long time ago, maybe in the late thirties."

The woman chewed on her lower lip in a thoughtful pose. She turned to her fellow worker. "Hey, Mona, didn't you look up a Jerome LeClaire for that guy yesterday—you know, the 'one you were ready to throw yourself at?''

The other woman, a short, slightly overweight brunette, joined them at the counter. ''What're you talking about me for? You were just as bad. He was something to see.'' She got a faraway look in her eyes. ''You know, I went to just about every bar in town last night trying to find that guy.''

The other woman bubbled over with a giggly laugh. ''Get out of here. And what were you going to do if you found him?''

Mona opened her eyes wide. ''I hadn't planned that far ahead.'' The two laughed together.

Ellie looked from one to the other. She was still reeling from the news that someone else had asked for information on Jerome LeClaire. The coincidence seemed too much to imagine. The redhead, realizing the two were not presenting their best side to a customer, recovered her decorum. ''Sorry about that, but you should have seen him. You don't see too many guys around here that look that gorgeous. Mostly we get old cowboys who've been on a horse too long.''

Mona chided her coworker. ''Now you know that's not true.''

''Well, pretty nearly,'' the redhead insisted.

Ellie ignored their dispute. ''You're sure about the name? Jerome LeClaire? Somebody was asking about *him*?''

Mona took over. ''Oh, yeah, that was it all right. Kind of a funny spelling.'' She spelled the name LeClaire and Ellie nodded. ''I found something, too. Anything to make *him* happy.'' She smiled again, but this time she kept it much more restrained. ''I think I remember the details, but I'll look it up again for you to be sure.'' She went to a large filing cabinet, pulled open the second drawer, and bent down to flip through the slips of paper yellowed with age. ''Here it is.'' She turned one of the slips on end to mark the place in the drawer and brought the requested item to the counter, turning it around for Ellie to read.

She read the address: 1501 Aspen Street. Then her eyes locked on one of the names listed—the same name appearing

on the stock certificate she had in her purse. So there really
was a Jerome LeClaire, and he really was from here. She
looked more closely at the notations typed at the bottom.
"What does all this mean?"

Mona had deciphered the same information just yesterday
for the handsome stranger, and she repeated it today for Ellie.
"The property was sold at auction by the county in September
of 1943 for nonpayment of taxes. It was owned by a Mary C.
LeClaire at the time. It doesn't say here, but I guess that was
Jerome's wife. I don't know if he died or what. The property
was sold to the city in 1953 by Harold Connors. The house
was torn down and the property was turned into a city park
the next year. Apparently the city must have acquired other
houses in the area because the park's good-sized. It's still
there, by the way. I can show it to you on the map if you
want to see it."

Ellie barely heard the woman's words after "nonpayment
of taxes." Obviously the guy hadn't made his fortune in the
oil fields if he couldn't pay the taxes on his house, she was
thinking. Even Grandpa's thousand dollars wasn't enough to
keep him afloat.

"It's right here." Mona had slipped a map of the town onto
the counter. She was pointing at a spot.

Ellie had a confused look on her face. "What?"

"The park. Where Jerome LeClaire's house was. It's right
here. And you're right about here now." She was designating
the courthouse with her other forefinger. "If you go down
Main right to this corner." She looked up. "It's still Aspen
Street just like it was then. The park is on the right, and the
way I figure it his house would have been right about here.
That's where the shelterhouse is. I didn't know that yesterday
when *he* was here. I figured it out from an old map after he
left." She turned to the redhead. "I wish I'd been able to tell
him that."

The other woman grinned. "Right. That's why you were
chasing all over town last night looking for him—so you could
tell him."

Mona ignored the remark and turned back to Ellie in all earnestness. "If you see him, tell him for me, will you?"

Ellie glanced up from the brilliant red fingernail marking a spot on the map. "What? Oh, sure, the shelterhouse. That's where the house was. I'll be sure to tell him if I see him." *Fat chance,* she thought. *He's probably long gone by now.* He was looking for an oil well, not a house. She took another glance at the name on the property record and stepped back from the counter. "Thanks so much. You've been very helpful."

"Oh, don't mention it," Mona said. "We're glad to help. It isn't often we get two requests like that one day after the other. By the way, I didn't ask him yesterday, but why would two of you be so all-fired interested in that name anyway? And after so long. I mean, it's none of our business. We're not supposed to ask or anything. But, you know, it is kind of a coincidence."

"No, that's all right," Ellie assured her. She chose her words carefully to keep the story short. "This Jerome LeClaire sold my grandfather some oil stock a long time ago, and I'm trying to track it down. I expect that's the same reason your gentleman friend was interested, too."

The redhead's eyes lighted. "Isn't that exciting! An oil well."

Ellie smiled. "The only problem is, it looks like Mr. LeClaire wasn't exactly striking it rich if he couldn't pay his taxes."

"Oh, that's so," Mona said with a flash of understanding. "I'm so sorry we had to give you bad news," she crooned sympathetically.

Ellie waved a hand. "Oh, that's all right. I wasn't expecting all that much, if you want to know the truth. But you know how it is. A person can dream. It would have been a long shot, about like winning the lottery. That's what one of my friends back home said, anyway."

"I expect you're right," Mona agreed. "That must have been why the gentleman yesterday seemed so disappointed. He was countin' on some hidden money, I bet. But from the looks of him, he wasn't bad off.'' She turned to her friend. ''Was he, Trish?''

The redhead, Trish, became animated. ''I guess so! His clothes were expensive, that's for sure. And did you see his watch? One of those real fancy ones.''

Ellie smiled at the office pair. ''Well, I'd better be going. Thanks again for all your help.''

The two women looked pleased with themselves behind the counter. ''That's all right,'' Mona said. ''We were glad to help. Just wish we'd had better news for you.''

Ellie made her way back out the heavy front door, down the steps, and across the street to her car. She slammed the door and sat weighing what she'd just heard. *Should I pack it in and head back to the Black Hills?* she asked herself. *Might just as well. Sounds like Jerome LeClaire was a loser. Unless . . .* She leaned back against the headrest thinking. The fact that he didn't pay his taxes doesn't prove anything really. He might have been just a general all-around sleeze. Didn't they say his wife was the one who was foreclosed on? Maybe he put it in her name so he could avoid the taxes. If he didn't mind taking money from Grandpa and probably lots of others and not pay it back, maybe he didn't mind ignoring other bills, too. Maybe he sold out his oil company and split. Her eyebrows arched with a sudden thought. Maybe that was why his wife got stuck with the bill. She made a decision. *As long as I'm here, I might as well find out the whole story.* She reached for the Howard Parker Museum flyer she'd tossed on the passenger seat and checked the map on its back for directions. *This is as good a place as any to try.* She started the car, slipped it in gear, and eased out of the parking space. She had gotten back at least half of her enthusiasm for the adventure, and though she would have denied it to anyone asking, at least part of the reason was the thought of a chance meeting with the office girls' Mr. Wonderful.

Ellie was disappointed when she spotted the Howard Parker Museum. It was located in a glass-front building that had once housed some kind of store. In fact, its next-door neighbor was a furniture refinishing shop. The parking was awkward, and she came very close to calling off the whole search when she thought again what a long shot it actually was. The door was open, though—it was becoming a warm day, and the building didn't seem to be air-conditioned from what she could tell—and so she walked on in. A young family—mother and father and two children, one a toddler and the other a boy of perhaps seven or eight—had the full attention of the young woman in charge. She was explaining something about a military encampment that had played a role in the town's past. The office area to the left was partitioned from the entryway by the backs of what Ellie guessed might be oak bookcases with a metal desk sandwiched in the middle. The young woman was standing behind this desk. Ellie saw no signs indicating a charge for admission, and she couldn't remember seeing anything about a charge on the brochure Lil, her motel friend, had given her, so she stepped past the family and down several steps to a long room which seemed to house most of the museum's displays.

The room smelled musty, not unlike one of Ellie's favorite places—an antique shop. There were rows of large glass cases on each side of a walkway, and she spotted what she was looking for in a second—an ancient photograph of an oil gusher spouting high over the top of a wooden rig. The photograph was inside one of the display cases on her left, and she began to move slowly around it, reading the information there. It was complete with maps and other photographs and even pieces of equipment from oil pumps and derricks. One picture caught her attention. It showed a group of workmen, smiles lighting their faces, standing under a gusher. Their clothes, their faces, even the ground around them were all soaked with the black gold. Ellie thought about what she had learned from Lil at breakfast about the depleted oil fields today. That the supply of oil would ever run out seemed the farthest thing from the minds of the men in the picture.

She moved further around the glass case, and her heart sank when she spotted a display of what was called, in bold lettering, worthless oil stock. It was done as a collage with the many official-looking documents arranged in an artistic way. She couldn't help but smile in spite of her disappointment when she thought of her own certificate tucked securely in her purse. If she had doubts before about its value, this display went a long way toward confirming those doubts. She read the accompanying explanation and discovered that Lil was right when she said that issuing shares of stock to finance oil exploration was commonplace. She bent close to the glass trying to spot a certificate like hers in the mix.

"Are you finding everything all right?"

Ellie jerked upright so quickly she felt a twinge of pain in her neck. She put a hand to her chest and let out a short laugh to try to cover her surprise.

"I'm sorry," the woman said. "I didn't mean to startle you."

Ellie studied the woman, who wasn't as young as she'd first thought. She seemed drained by the heat in the building, and her brown hair had gone limp with the humidity. "That's all right. I just didn't hear you come up. Was it all right to come on in? I didn't know if I needed to register or something."

"Oh, no, no, that's perfectly okay. We're very informal around here. Any questions I can answer?"

Ellie hesitated. "Well, as a matter of fact, I'm trying to research an oil stock issued to my grandfather a long time ago. This display seems to confirm what I've suspected all along—that it isn't worth the paper it's printed on."

The woman smiled, a very pleasant, understanding smile. She knew something about worthless oil stock. She was asked to check out old-time oil companies at least once or twice a week. "We have a file back in the office that includes a lot of the old oil companies. It might be a pretty good place to start. I'll be glad to check if you'd like."

"Thanks, that would be great. I just came from the courthouse, and I've lost most of my optimism, not that I had a lot to begin with, but I might as well get all of the bad news before I leave." She followed the woman back down the corridor between the glass cases toward the makeshift office. The woman slipped through a narrow opening between the desk and one of the partitions and turned to face Ellie. For the first time she noticed another woman, this one younger, pecking inexpertly at the keyboard of a computer just to the left of the main desk. Ellie could see the woman eying her over the top of the computer monitor. "Now, if you could give me some information, the name of a company or maybe the person issuing the stock."

Ellie dug for the certificate in her purse and laid it on the desk. "It's called the LeClaire Oil Syndicate, and the certificate is signed by Jerome LeClaire." She glanced up into a look of near-disbelief. "Don't tell me he's been *here,* too."

The woman recovered herself. "So you know about him?" She seemed relieved that there must be a logical explanation for such a coincidence.

"I know *about* him, but I don't *know* him. I was at the courthouse before I came here, and he'd been there yesterday." She lifted an eyebrow. "And left quite an impression, I might add."

The woman's light complexion reddened. "He really was quite handsome." Her look was wistful. "He had such a pleasant smile."

"And the rest of him wasn't bad, either," came a voice from behind the computer.

The first woman shot a look toward the computer. "Karen," she said, "of all the things to say."

The hunting and pecking stopped and the other woman stretched higher in her chair so Ellie could see her more clearly. She was in her early twenties, dark-haired, quite thin. "Well, it's the truth," she said. "All you can talk about is his smile, but he's flat-out good-looking, I can tell you. Kind of like a movie star or something. Very sophisticated." Suddenly she turned her head and raised her chin in a perfect imitation of the first woman's bearing and said in an overly dramatic voice, "He really was quite handsome."

"Karen," the first woman said sharply, "would you stop that."

Ellie could only guess the two were on an even footing in

this office. She couldn't imagine a subordinate making fun of her boss in such an obvious way.

The first woman became very businesslike to cover her embarrassment at the slight that had just been inflicted. ''The fact of the matter is it's surprising to have two people ask about the same name over the course of less than twenty-four hours. In fact, it's never happened before. Now, you'll be interested to know I did find some information about a Jerome LeClaire, not much, but some. At least it seemed to interest the young man who was here yesterday. Let me just find that file. I think I know exactly where it is.'' She scurried to one of the file cabinets in the center of the room.

Ellie glanced in the direction of the computer mainly to satisfy her curiosity about why it hadn't started up again and saw Karen staring at her, a broad grin spread across her thin face. Ellie didn't know what to make of the look, and she glanced away quickly just as the first woman returned with two file folders. ''Yes, here they are. I'm afraid they won't be of much help, but at least they tell you there *was* a LeClaire Oil Company, and it apparently was active in the fields. Not for very long, though. The company became LeClaire/Whitiker in 1938, and that's about all I have here. I pulled the Whitiker file, too. There was a Whitiker Oil that emerged in 1942. It would appear that Whitiker must have bought out Mr. LeClaire about that time. Then in 1945 Whitiker was purchased by Lassiter Petroleum. They're still doing business. As a matter of fact, they're one of the biggest around. If you drove in from the east, you would have seen their offices just on the edge of town.'' Ellie nodded, remembering the office building and maintenance yard she'd seen yesterday. ''You're welcome to look these over if they would be of any help.'' She slid the two folders forward on the desk.

Ellie opened each in turn and scrutinized what was inside. It was all there, what the woman had told her. She was very thorough, but, of course, Ellie remembered, she'd been through it twice in as many days. She handed the folders back. ''Thanks. You've been very helpful.''

''That's quite all right. We're glad to help. Now if you'd

like to pursue this further, you might check at Lassiter Petroleum. They actually have very good records of the history of the oil find around here, mainly because they've been here almost from the beginning.'' She tapped the folders in front of her. ''And they *did* buy out Whitiker, and Whitiker bought out LeClaire, so there is a connection. Whether they would honor your claim or not, I have my doubts.''

Ellie smiled. ''So do I.'' She held up the document between thumb and forefinger. ''Not worth the paper it's printed on, as they say. Though I think I'll frame it. It makes a good conversation piece, don't you think?'' She slipped it back in her purse.

The woman smiled. ''That's what some people do, I know.''

''Which brings up a point.'' Ellie wondered out loud, ''Do any of these certificates ever prove to be worth anything?''

''Not to my knowledge. At least not now. I expect if a person had made a claim not long after the transaction, there might have been a chance. But from what I understand that wasn't necessary with a reputable company. It was the fly-by-nights that caused the problem. They collected the money, and that's all they cared about. I don't think they ever intended to drill a well.''

Ellie smiled ruefully. ''I've got a pretty good idea that's what happened in this case. So did you tell *him* about Whitiker?''

''As a matter of fact, I did. I also told him to check at the library. It probably wouldn't interest you, but he seemed to want to find out what happened to this LeClaire fellow. They have copies of the town paper on file at the library. It was real folksy then.'' She laughed. ''Come to think of it, it's still pretty folksy, if you want to know the truth. Anyway, you might find out some personal information going back through the paper.''

Ellie turned to go. ''Well, thanks again. I wouldn't mind catching up with this guy if he's as hunky as you say he is.'' She glanced toward the computer and arched her eyebrows.

Karen grinned over the monitor. "He is. I'm tellin' you the truth. If you find him, tell him hi from me."

"I'll do that," Ellie said with a laugh, and she headed out the open door.

Once back in the car, she checked her watch. It was just a little before 11:00. Plenty of time to pay a visit to Lassiter Petroleum before the lunch hour would make finding someone to talk to difficult. She drove slowly back through downtown in the direction of the highway she'd taken yesterday. She knew Lassiter Petroleum was on that highway because she'd seen it on the way in. She thought about the mystery man as she drove along. What were the odds, she wondered, that someone else could be researching the same name after sixty years? She wished she could meet him, not just to satisfy her curiosity about a man who had left four women salivating, but also to find out his story. Was his claim an old family thing? Someone digging round in an old trunk somewhere found a yellowed certificate, like the one she had in her purse, and he was picked to investigate it? That they should both be searching for the same person at the same time she found positively incredible. He must be gone by now, she decided. He'd been a day ahead, and he hadn't found out anything that would encourage him to hang around. It should have been obvious to any semi-intelligent person that Jerome LeClaire never amounted to anything in the oil game.

She stopped at a red light and raked her right hand through her hair. Unless, of course, he made off with investors' money to try again somewhere else and left his wife holding the bag here and she had to sell out to this Whitiker fellow because there wasn't any money left to do any more drilling. She laughed out loud at the absurdity of her little scenario. *Ellie Regan, you are totally impossible,* she thought to herself. *If Grandpa had an imagination like mine, no wonder he got taken in by some scam artist.*

The light changed, and she continued on her way, her brain still mulling over what she had learned so far. No, the only possible way any old oil shares could be worth anything, she decided, was if the shares in LeClaire followed to Whitiker and then to Lassiter. Fat chance of that, though. *And anyway, how would I prove it after all these years? So what am I hoping to find out at Lassiter Petroleum, anyway? The woman said they have complete records of everything that went on around here, but I don't even know what records to look for.* A high, chainlink fence appeared suddenly on her left, and she recognized the office building and expanse of maintenance yards she'd passed on the way into town. She pulled into the parking lot by the office and slipped her Toyota into one of the four stalls designated by four neat signs as visitor parking. One of the visitor stalls was occupied, and she took the spot one over leaving a space in between.

She switched off the ignition and sat for a minute trying to collect her thoughts and decide what to do. *Should I just call off this silliness?* she asked herself. *I've found out about what I expected to, anyway.* She glanced toward the building. *I can't imagine what else they can tell me in here.* She was only vaguely aware, by a glint of reflected sun, that the glass front door opened and someone came out. *If I hurry, I can make it to the motel before noon checkout and get serious about a little sight-seeing. Anyway, I gave it the old college try.* Her eyes drifted to the car on her left at the sound of the door opening. A man looked her way as he stepped into the car. All she saw was a face, a very handsome face with a strong, confident jaw, chiseled features, and a shock of unruly, light-brown hair. "Could that be him?" she asked out loud. As the car backed out, she watched for the license plate. Wyoming. *Hmm, maybe not.* Then she spotted the Hertz sticker on the bumper. *That's got to be him,* she said, this time to herself. She started her car and flung it into reverse. She reached the parking lot entrance as he pulled from the frontage road back onto the highway toward town. She had to wait for a truck, then pulled out just behind it. She waited her chance, then slipped around the truck and took her place a safe distance behind his car.

Her heart was beating wildly with excitement. *What in heaven's name am I doing? I haven't done anything like this*

*since I was in high school. I'm probably jumping to a huge
conclusion that's it's him. All I've got to go on is they said
he's got to-die-for looks, and this guy seemed to fit that description from what I saw.* They were coming closer to the
heart of town, and she was trying to calm herself. *Now what
do I do? Am I going to have to run him down to get his
attention?* He signaled for a right turn, and she followed close
behind. He pulled into a parking spot not far from the restaurant Ellie had tried last night. *He's stopping for lunch.* She
slowed and looked frantically for a parking space of her own.
*Just my luck this has to be the most popular place in town.
Probably the only place.* She saw a parking spot halfway
down the block and sped up to reach it. She pulled in, yanked
on the brake, and scrambled out. She could see him sauntering
toward the front door. *What am I going to say? What am I
going to say?*

Gasping for breath, she reached the door a second before
him. He smiled as he stopped to let her pass. ''I'm not going
in,'' she said, knowing as she said them how odd her words
must sound to him.

He gave her a quizzical look. ''Oh? Well, if you'll excuse
me, I am.''

Realizing he was waiting for her to move, she blurted, ''No,
you see I need to talk to you.''

His look was still one of confusion. ''Do I know you?''

''Well, no, not exactly. But I think you're the one I've been
following around all morning. No, that isn't exactly right either. What I mean is every place I went this morning you'd
already been there. Or at least I think it was you.''

Even though the young woman blocking his way was most
attractive, she wasn't making any sense. ''Look, I don't know
what you're talking about, but if this is some kind of come-
on, I'm not interested.'' He started to move past her.

Her mouth gaped in surprise. ''Some kind of come-on? You
think I'm . . .'' Her words trailed off as she realized he thought
she was flirting with him. ''Why, of all the nerve!'' She was
suddenly furious. How could he imagine she would throw her-

self at him like that? "You must have a pretty inflated opinion of yourself."

The tone of anger in her voice stopped him cold. Maybe he *had* misjudged her. He tried to soften his voice, but he couldn't quite keep a hard edge of impatience from accompanying his words. "Well, what is it then? What is it you want?"

Ellie took a deep breath to gather herself. She drew herself up to her full five-foot-seven height and looked him squarely in the eye. This time she would select her words more carefully and make sense, or she'd know the reason why. "All right, here's the deal. I'm trying to find out if we're looking for the same information. I've been to the courthouse and the town museum asking about Jerome LeClaire, and everyone I talk to says there'd already been someone there yesterday asking the same questions. I find that all pretty surprising since this all happened over sixty years ago. So, I just followed you across town from Lassiter Petroleum because I thought you might be the one who's been asking about him. Now, if I have the wrong person, then I'm terribly sorry." She'd said her piece and was out of breath. Now she stood staring up at him with the quizzical look on *her* face.

His calm detachment had changed completely at the first mention of the name LeClaire. In fact, he hadn't heard much of what she'd said after that. Now it was his turn to gape. "I'm sorry, did I hear you correctly? Did you say Jerome LeClaire?"

"That's exactly what I said," she answered with a show of confidence. She'd been afraid of making a fool of herself by approaching the wrong man. Now she was sure he was the one who had left the women at the courthouse and the museum in such a state. "So, then it *was* you who's been checking around about him?"

He ignored the question. "How do you know about Jerome LeClaire?"

"The same way you do, I imagine. I'm assuming we're here for the same reason. I've got a piece of worthless oil stock right here in my purse signed by good old Jerome

LeClaire." She patted the purse which was hanging from her shoulder. "The guy scammed my grandfather out of one thousand dollars over sixty years ago, and I'm out here trying to find out what happened to that money." She studied him expectantly, waiting for a sign of understanding, a smile maybe, some reaction to this unbelievable coincidence that they were both investigating ancient wrongs to family members from the same person. But she didn't get it. She watched his face and saw the surprise there for sure, maybe shock would be more like it at first, then some strange sign of understanding, and finally something she certainly hadn't expected—anger.

They both had to step aside to let a couple get to the door of the restaurant. As they squared off again on the sidewalk, his look had become more a glare. It became immediately obvious he hadn't really heard everything she'd said. "Let me guess. Now you're going to be willing to settle the whole business for a hundred bucks." His tone was sarcastic. "Too high? Maybe fifty is more your speed. Listen, I don't know who you are or what you're trying to pull, but if you don't get lost I'm going to call the cops. Who tipped you off I was looking for information about my grandfather? Somebody at the courthouse? The museum? Nice friendly town! I *should* call the cops. Do you ever find anybody stupid enough to fall for a scam like this? Like I'd be willing to pay up for something my grandfather supposedly did sixty years ago? What do you do, just hang around looking for tourists?" He turned abruptly, strode for the door, and entered the restaurant.

The door slammed behind him, but not before her next questioning words followed at almost a shout—"*Your grandfather?!*"

Now it was Ellie's turn to register anger as she stood outside the restaurant, but there was no one left for her to vent it at. *He thinks* I'm *the one who's trying to pull a scam. How could he think such a thing? What did I say that made him think anything of the sort?* Then his words sank in. *Jerome LeClaire is his grandfather? This is all just too strange.* She should have followed him through the door, gone to his table, and straightened him out right then and there. At least that's what she told herself the rest of the afternoon. In fact, she even tried to do just that but not right away. She went back to her car, her head spinning, still smarting from his ridiculous accusations. She drove aimlessly around the tiny town trying to calm herself, for how long she really wasn't certain. Finally, spotting a fast-food place, she went inside and ordered a burger and fries. She was midway through the burger when she decided what she had to do—what she should have done in the first place. She hurried to her car and drove back to the restaurant. Her heart sank when she noticed his car was gone, but she went inside anyway. She stood at the front scanning the tables until the hostess approached her. "Table for one?"

"No, no, I've already eaten. I'm looking for someone. I know he came in here. About six-foot-one, brown hair, good-looking. He was wearing brown slacks, a camel-colored sports jacket, a light, crewneck shirt." She was surprised at herself, even a little embarrassed that she had such a precise description of him.

The woman gave her a thin, knowing smile. "Of course. I can see why you might be looking for him. He was here all right. You just missed him. He sat at the third table by the window." She pointed toward a table that was being reset. "Ate in a hurry and left, oh, maybe ten minutes ago."

Ellie smiled feebly, thanked the woman, and hurried out the door.

Graham Stahmers heard the young woman's words follow as the door slammed behind him. He fully expected the door to fly open and the woman to be standing there ready to confront him again. He walked quickly to an empty table near a window and sat facing the door ready for her. But she didn't come, and he ordered quickly off the daily selections posted at each table. He replayed the whole strange confrontation in his mind while he was waiting for his food, and it was then he began to think he might have misjudged the pretty young woman. He had to admit when he heard her mention his grandfather's name, nothing much registered after that. What was it she said? Something about "we're here for the same reason?'' What did she mean? She said she had an oil stock with her. *She never really asked for money, and she certainly got all upset when I accused her of trying to con me out of some bucks.* He thought of the words that followed him through the door. There was no mistaking what she said— ''Your *grandfather?!*'' Everybody there heard it. He remembered how they all turned toward the door. He remembered clearly how she said it as a question. Yes, he had misjudged her.

By the time the waitress had slipped his salad in front of him, he thought he had things figured out. It was obvious she had a worthless piece of stock signed by his grandfather. Could that be? Was his grandfather the type who made his money dealing phony oil stocks? How should he know? He'd never laid eyes on the man, knew absolutely nothing about him. After all, that's why he was out here, trying to track down some trace of him for his mother. He realized suddenly that this young woman might hold a clue to his grandfather's past. Maybe not a clue he would be happy about, but a clue nonetheless. He left his salad untasted and hurried for the door. He stepped outside and looked up and down the street for her, realizing the absurdity that she would still be hanging around after the brush-off he'd given her. He stepped back inside, and the hostess he'd missed the first time around stepped toward him with a worried look on her face. ''Sir, is there a problem?''

''No, no, it's nothing,'' he mumbled without really satisfying her curiosity. He returned to the table and finished his meal hurriedly. He walked to his car wondering what his next move should be in the search for his past, and cursing himself for scaring off a woman who might have helped him put some of the missing pieces together.

Chapter Four

Ellie drove slowly back to the motel. It was already well past the checkout time, so she would stay another night here and then move back east toward the Black Hills for her sightseeing. *I've had it with oil well chasing after the morning I've been through,* she decided. But she wasn't really all that surprised that the oil stock was worthless. *That's about what I was expecting all along,* she thought. *But being one step behind that guy, whose name I don't even know,* she reminded herself, *was exciting enough. Almost like some movie. Too bad he had to turn out to be such a royal pain,* she thought to herself. She smiled as she decided how she would tell her friends. "I met Prince Charming on my trip except he wasn't a prince and he sure wasn't charming," she rehearsed out loud. *Nikki will like that. She'll be crazy about the whole story, come to think of it. They all will. Maybe not Jan. Oh, she'll like it well enough, but she'll think I made it up. The part about somebody else looking for Jerome LeClaire, too. I doubt if I'd believe it, either, if I hadn't seen him with my own two eyes. I can hardly wait to tell them all. It's just too bad it turned out the way it did. It would have made a much better story if he'd been halfway human about it all. If I had a friend who was a lawyer, it would be a blast to work up a claim against that guy.* The new idea brought an nasty grin to her face. *Who could I get to do that?* Just a letter would be good enough, an official-sounding letter loaded with legal mumbo jumbo. Then a sobering thought struck her. *Aren't you forgetting something? You don't even know his name.*

Back at the motel, she went to her room to decide what to do for the afternoon and evening of her last day here. She had always wanted to see Devils Tower, especially from what she saw of it in the old movie *Close Encounters of the Third Kind,* and from the looks of the map it wasn't too far to the north. She would go there this afternoon and then leave early the next morning for Rapid City and the Black Hills. She went to the office to find a brochure on Devils Tower.

Lil was on duty. Her eyes brightened when Ellie came through the door. "I was just thinkin' about ya. So did ya strike it rich this morning?"

Ellie smiled. "Don't I wish. No, looks like I'm going to have to make my money the old-fashioned way—I'll have to earn it."

The woman's ready laugh brought on a mild coughing fit requiring the tissue up her sleeve. "That's about what I figured," she said with a knowing smile.

"But he did have an oil company," Ellie hurriedly added so the woman wouldn't get away with thinking this whole business was a pipe dream. "So he wasn't lying about that. The only trouble was, it didn't last very long. He had to sell out." She didn't share the great coincidence about meeting the man's grandson, because she was positive it would bring on one of Lil's laughs again. "You were right about the museum. They couldn't have been more helpful there."

Lil was pleased. "I told ya they'd treat ya right there. So what now, little lady? Is that about all for the fortune hunting?"

"I'm afraid so. I'm going back to the Black Hills in the morning. I thought I'd drive up to Devils Tower this afternoon. I've always wanted to see it, and I might as well as long as I'm in the neighborhood. I was wondering if you might have something on it."

The woman hurried to the rack of brochures. "I most certainly do. Right here." She pulled a brochure out of its slot and handed it to Ellie. "But ya don't want to go there this time a day."

Ellie was studying the eerie, misty photo of the flat-topped tower on the front of the literature Lil had handed her. It reminded her all over again of the strange scene in *Close Encounters* when Richard Dreyfuss, acting out of some compulsion, fashioned a replica of the tower out of clay in his house. She looked up in surprise as Lil's words finally came through. "Why?"

" 'Cause it looks better in the morning," the woman said as if her pronouncement was common knowledge to anyone who knew anything. She pointed at the picture Ellie was holding. "If ya wanta see it like that, ya gotta go in the morning. The sun's too bright on it in the afternoon. It just stands out there lookin' like a sore thumb. Besides, ya go now, ya'll have to fight about twenty thousand people and their kids fallin' all over theirselves tryin' to see it." She was emphatic. "No, ya wanta go early in the morning. That's when it's best."

Ellie was thinking out loud. "I guess I could pack and go up there in the morning and then head on to Rapid City. That would work, wouldn't it?"

Lil nodded. "Right you are. The interstate highway's not more'n a stone's throw from Devils Tower, and that'll take ya straight into Rapid City."

"My only problem now is what to do with the rest of the afternoon."

The woman screwed her face up into a look that would have stopped a car in the street. "Little lady, Lil's got a whole rack of stuff for you to do." She waved in the direction of her array of brochures. "Now let me see." She walked to the rack and began sifting through the material. "How are you and ghost towns?"

Ellie shrugged. "I don't know. Guess I've never been to one."

Lil looked at her for all the world like a crotchety teacher addressing a student who'd neglected her homework. "Well, we're goin' to take care of that hole in your education right here and now." She pulled a brochure and opened it on the counter. "This here town's called Maryville. I'll show ya the best way to get there from here."

Ellie was beginning to feel powerless around the woman, and she stepped forward to follow the gnarled forefinger as it traced the route out of town. She couldn't resist a comment that she knew would get a reaction. "I thought the best time to visit a ghost town was the middle of the night."

Lil stepped away from the counter, cocked her head to one side, and shot another of her looks. Ellie smiled at the theatrics. She was beginning to like this woman. "You're welcome to go there in the dead of night if ya want to, but ya wouldn't catch me out in one of them spooky places at night for all the tea in China. And I mean it." She turned her attention again to the brochure on the counter. "Now, this place was an old coal town a long time ago. The coal's all gone or, more likely, too hard to come by now, so everything's just sittin' the way it was the day they all left. It's kinda spooky, like I was sayin', but not half bad in broad daylight." She refolded the literature and slapped it in Ellie's hand. "If ya leave right this minute, ya should have plenty of time to poke around. Take some water, though," she cautioned. "It's mighty hot out today."

Ellie had little choice but do as she was told, and anyway the trip looked interesting. She dug her backpack out of the trunk of the car, filled her canteen with ice and water, and tossed in a few snacks from the convenience store just down the street. And she was off. Getting there was half the fun, as it turned out. Following the map Lil had outlined for her, she traveled dusty, gravel roads west of the town through great expanses of grass gently swaying in the wind. She saw herds of cattle and a few antelope and a handful of oil pumpers, but most of those weren't working. She drove for a time among low hills, missed a turn in the road because a sign was nearly covered by high grass, and had to backtrack about three miles when she finally realized her mistake. And she might never have known she'd taken a wrong turn if the road hadn't begun to narrow perceptibly until she was guiding her wheels down not much more than two ruts overgrown with weeds. But in the length of time it took her brain to convince her it was time to turn around, even those ruts had given way to a field of car-roof-high grass. She backed the Toyota carefully into a tight semicircle, leery of what holes might be lurking in the tall grass, and made her way back to the comfort of the road. She drove slowly, looking closely for where she might have gone wrong until she spotted the sign partially obscured by grass.

Relieved to be on the right track again, she headed up a long, gentle rise and just at the top the road took a sharp left turn, and she was there. Or, at least, she assumed she was there. A half dozen cars were parked haphazardly in a field to her right, and she pulled the Toyota in to join them. She climbed out and dug in the back seat for her backpack, hoisting it to her shoulders before donning her wide-brimmed explorer's hat. Then she was off hiking a mostly untended trail through what once must have been the thriving town of Maryville. The path wound among deteriorating cabins with their broken windows, missing roofs, and the odd piece of furniture. Then the trail left the town itself and climbed the hills behind it, another half-mile or so, to what had been the busy mine. She passed rusted-out trucks and the remains of pieces of mining equipment whose purpose she could only guess at. It was obvious Lil was right. The place had been abandoned almost as if on a single command. It looked like workers had just walked away one day.

She met or passed only a few other hikers, the ones belonging to the cars in the makeshift parking lot. She smiled to herself. *I wonder if Lil has ever been to this place? Or does she rely on those little brochures of hers for all her sightseeing?* She sat on a fallen log and dug in her backpack for a candy bar. She took a long sip of water and looked down over the remains of the town which she could see pretty clearly from her vantage point. The sight depressed her. She knew why, too. The houses reminded her of her own grandparents' farmhouse that she'd seen, probably for the last time, just two days earlier. She knew those houses down there, just as with that crumbling Iowa home, had once been filled with the hopes and dreams of the men and women and children inside them. The thought made her sad. They were all dead now, probably dead for years and years.

The stunning revelation she'd learned in front of the restaurant a few hours earlier, never far from her mind all afternoon, drifted into her thoughts again. *I wonder how old this town is? Sixty or seventy years? Probably not much older than that. That means* his *grandfather was living around here when this town was alive. Grandpa and Grandma weren't any older than I am now.* The thought of them so young and so alive brought sudden tears to her eyes. She had such an odd feeling just then that a chill ran up her spine and down her arms. She slid her hands up each arm and hugged herself in a gesture she might use to keep warm on a cold day. She even felt goose bumps on her arms, though the afternoon had turned hot as Lil predicted. She felt a certain closeness with the past that she'd never experienced before.

Maybe that's what ghost towns are supposed to do to you, she thought. *That's why Lil says you shouldn't come out here in the middle of the night,* she decided, in a weak attempt to dismiss the strange feeling. But her brain insisted on getting to the bottom of things. *I feel like I've got some kind of a weird tie to this place somehow. I've got Grandpa's oil stock which must have meant a lot more to him than anyone knew. Otherwise he would have joked about it. That's the way he was about everything, always joking, always finding something to laugh about. But not about the oil stock. It's signed by a man who lived right around here. Maybe he had friends in this town.* She glanced down the hill. *For all I know, he might have walked down that street. I wonder if he ever thought about Grandpa again after he drove away with his thousand dollars in his pocket?*

And what about all the other people he made his pitch to along the way? Did he ever intend to pay any of them back? Was he really selling them an interest in an oil well, or did he just set out to rip them off from the very beginning? *I wonder what he was like.* Grandpa didn't seem to be the gullible sort. Maybe he was before he met up with good old Jerome LeClaire. The dream of finding a fortune in a Wyoming oil well had pretty much disappeared for Ellie in the last ten hours or so, not that she ever really believed it would happen, anyway. What was left in place of the dream were questions, lots of them, and she had little chance of finding the answers.

That thought brought her back to the stranger from the restaurant. *If he hadn't been such a jerk, I might have found out something. Why didn't I march into that restaurant and create such a scene he'd have to tell me everything he knew about his grandfather?* She shook her head for at least the fifteenth time this afternoon at the thought of the lost opportunity. Not that the guy made it any easier with his accusations. *Of course, I didn't waste any time telling him his grandfather was a crook. One of my usual foot-in-mouth operations. So how was I supposed to know it was his grandfather? That is so incredible.* She propped an elbow on each knee and cradled her chin in her hands. A smile stole across her face. *Those women at the courthouse and the museum were right. He* is *cute. Cute nothing, he's gorgeous. And I don't even know his name. Well, how about LeClaire. Could be, couldn't it?*

She wrinkled her forehead. *I wonder if I went back to the courthouse and the museum if they'd know his name. They never mentioned it, but then I didn't ask. You'd think that if his name* was *LeClaire like his grandfather, they would have said something about it. Yes, I'm certain they would have. His name must be something different, and now I'll never know. Ellie Regan,* she scolded herself, *would you just drop it. You're checking out tomorrow morning early, and that's final. You came out here to check on a lost oil well, and now you know it never existed, so let it go at that.* On that note of resolution, she stood up, slipped her arms through the straps of her backpack, and headed off down the hill toward her car.

Ellie was in the motel office for the continental breakfast so early the next morning that Lil hadn't come on duty yet. The pastry was fresher at such an early hour, but she missed the sharp-tongued woman's take on life in general. She had hoped to say good-bye before pulling out, but she wanted to get to

Devils Tower as early as possible to take advantage of the morning light that Lil described as so important. The drive took her through more rolling hills of grassland with the occasional herd of cattle gathered for a morning drink at a tank fed by its churning windmill. There were more oil pumpers visible, and most of these, unlike the ones she'd seen yesterday, were working away, bowing their heads to the ground in their rhythmic way.

She first caught sight of the famous tower while she was still maybe fifteen miles away. It wasn't as dramatic as, say, first seeing the mountains, she decided, but it was still impressive in a strange sort of way. It was such an oddly shaped thing, with its straight sides and flat top. And there wasn't much else around it to get in its way. The drive had taken nearly an hour and a half, and she wasn't as early as she'd hoped. It was a little after 8:00, but the morning fog hadn't been completely burned off and was hugging the base of the tower. She paid her entrance fee to a sleepy ranger at the kiosk and proceeded up the winding road to the visitor center. She managed a sharp hairpin in the road and slammed on the brakes. A doe and her tiny fawn were edging carefully across the hard surface to the underbrush on the other side. The pair stopped to stare, and Ellie did the same. As they moved off, she continued slowly on her way.

The parking areas weren't crowded at this hour, but they weren't exactly empty, either. She guessed Lil might be right that the place could be wall-to-wall tourists later in the day. She parked and pulled her trusty backpack out of the car. She had every intention of taking the hike around the base of the tower. She made her way to the visitor center and stood for a long moment, shading her eyes and craning her neck to study the tower from top to bottom before she stepped inside the log building to browse through the displays, intent on orienting herself before taking her hike.

She read first the Indian legend about the place. She'd seen the story in Lil's brochure, but she enjoyed it a second time. Seven girls, so the story went, climbed onto a rock in their attempt to escape a bear chasing them. They began to pray to the rock to save them, and the rock, hearing their prayers, grew upward, toward the sky, with the bear clawing at its sides as he scrambled to reach them. His claw marks, according to the legend, created the deep gashes in the side of the tower visible to this day.

Next Ellie studied a display providing the geological explanation for the strange formation. She learned the unusual tower, whose base she could just make out through the window of the visitor center when she glanced away from the display case, was once the core of a volcano which filled with molten lava and hardened as it cooled. Her brain struggled with the thought of the millions of years needed to erode the area around the volcano's core to leave the tower as it was today. The claw marks of legend, she read, were created when the core cooled faster than the area around it and cracked into five-sided shafts of rock. Over millions of years some of these shafts had crumbled off leaving long grooves down the sides.

There were other displays, but Ellie decided to save them for later. She was anxious to see close up the grooves she'd been reading about, and she hurried outside and across the road to the trail head to begin her hike. She'd been carrying her backpack slung over her shoulder, and she slipped her arms through the straps. One of the straps refused to lie flat over her shoulder, and she stopped for just an instant to adjust it, unaware that she was blocking the view of a man, camera to his eye, preparing to snap a picture. Catching sight of him out of the corner of her eye just as she conquered the strap, she hopped quickly out of his line of fire. "Excuse me," she said, and just then his camera lowered, and their eyes met. "It's you!"

"You took the words right out of my mouth," he replied in a not unfriendly tone. At least it was more than Ellie would have expected after their abrupt parting of the day before. Neither of them spoke for a moment, long enough for her to complete a quick appraisal. He was wearing gray walking shorts, hiking boots, and a light-yellow cotton T-shirt that contoured nicely to his well-developed shoulders and arms. His legs were muscular and sturdy, the legs of a runner or at least a jogger, she surmised. He was wearing a canvas safari hat similar to her own, but it was perched on the back of his head at what she thought was an odd angle until she realized he'd probably pushed it back like that to make room for his camera so the brim of the hat wouldn't get in the way of the lens. The camera dangled from a strap just below his chest, and she noticed that the camera was a complicated-looking thing with a long lens and adjustments completely foreign to the simple point-and-shoot she had stuffed in her backpack. She took all of this in in a matter of seconds until she focused on his face and found herself locked in a gaze with a pair of the darkest eyes she could remember ever seeing.

"So, we meet again," he said with a smile, a very engaging smile.

"Yes, it would appear so," she replied in what she knew was a lame response, but it was the best she could manage under the circumstances.

"I want to apologize for the things I said to you yesterday. It's just that you caught me by surprise."

"No, no, I should be the one apologizing." Even as she said these words she wasn't so sure she meant them, at least not one hundred percent. After all, unless she'd completely misunderstood him, he had at least accused her of being some kind of local scam artist. But then hadn't she suggested his grandfather was a crook? And she *had* sprung at him in the street like some kind of stalker. There was blame on both sides. "I shouldn't have said those things about your grandfather. But, of course, I didn't know I was talking about your grandfather!" The oddity of it all had crashed in on her again. "Your grandfather! I still can't believe it."

He smiled. She definitely liked his smile, she decided. "You couldn't have been any more surprised than I was to hear you mention his name." They were still standing practically in the middle of the road, and a pickup towing a trailer squealed to a stop in front of them, the driver scowling impatiently through the windshield. "We'd better move before we get turned into road kill," he said with a laugh. They edged toward the shoulder of the road. "There's a bench over there,'' he said. ''Do you mind sitting for a few minutes? I must admit I'm dying to find out what you know about my grandfather.''

They walked toward the bench and sat. Aware that he was looking at her, waiting for what she could tell him, she began, ''I'm afraid you're going to be disappointed. I know next to nothing about your grandfather.''

''You're sure? I promise you can tell me anything, and I won't so much as raise an eyebrow. You just caught me by surprise yesterday.''

She smiled. ''No, really, I don't know all that much about him. No, that's not quite right. I don't know *anything* about him.''

''But what about the oil stock you mentioned?''

''The long and short of it is this,'' she began. ''A man by the name of Jerome LeClaire drove into my grandfather's farmyard in Iowa back in 1939. He sold Grandpa some oil stock for a thousand dollars, got back in his car, and drove away. That obviously was the last time the two ever saw each other. My dad died last year, and my mom and I found the stock among his papers. He found it when his dad, my grandfather, died some fifteen years ago. It was stuck away in an old rolltop desk. My dad used to joke about the stock after he found it, but he never tried to find out anything about it as far as I know. Apparently Grandpa was always tight-lipped about it. All I know about it was what Dad found out from Grandma after Grandpa died. She said he always felt foolish for giving a perfect stranger a thousand dollars. In cash, no less. All they had at the time,'' she said emphatically.

''He never tried to find out what happened to his money?''

''According to Grandma he wrote a letter to Mr. LeClaire about two years later,'' Ellie explained, ''but it was returned because he didn't have a complete address or something. The stock certificate just lists a county but no town or other address. Then he went to war, and when he came back, he must have figured it was too late. Or else he just decided he'd been taken for the money, and there wasn't much sense in trying to do anything about it. He was like that. You know, kind of

a stoic about some things.'' She held her hands out palms up
in a gesture of apology almost. ''That's all I know. Honest.''

Obviously disappointed, he slipped a strap for his camera
bag off his shoulder. She hadn't noticed the case until now.
He unzipped it and stowed his camera. He went through these
actions automatically, like a robot, his eyes never moving
from a spot somewhere off in the distance. As she watched
him waiting for a reaction, she shrugged out of her backpack
so she could sit more comfortably. She was beginning to wonder if he was ever going to say anything more to her or if she
should slip away and continue her exploration, when he pulled
an ankle up to rest on one knee and finally looked her way as
if he suddenly realized she was still sitting next to him.
''Sorry, didn't mean to space out on you. I was just thinking.
I came a thousand miles out here to try to uncover my grandfather's past, and what do I find? He was a swindler. People
back home warned me about poking around in your ancestors'
graves. You never know what you're going to find out. I
would have been better off staying at home.'' He laughed a
short, harsh laugh, one that didn't seem to fit with what little
Ellie knew of the man. ''It's almost funny, isn't it?''

She didn't know if he expected an answer. Half of her was
wishing she'd acted on her impulse of a few minutes earlier
and gone away by herself to hike around the tower. When she
finally spoke, her words were no longer accusing. ''You don't
know for sure he was a swindler,'' she said. ''He might have
been intending to pay the money back but never got around
to it.'' Even as she said these things, she knew they sounded
lame. He gave her a look that suggested he thought about as
much. She didn't even understand herself this sudden rush to
defend a man she'd decided long ago had wronged her grandfather, and she wasn't finished yet. ''No, I mean it,'' she went
on. ''What do you really know? Do you know when he died?''

He shook his head. ''Not really.''

''Well, for all you know,'' she said as if she were certain
it was so, ''he might have died before he had a chance to pay
the money back.''

He smiled. ''That's possible, but it's also possible he was

in the business of swindling.'' He shifted on the bench. ''Listen,'' he said in a tone that suggested he wanted to change the subject. ''I need to make a little confession.'' Ellie studied him with arched eyebrows, wondering what was coming. ''You know yesterday when I stormed by you into that restaurant?'' She nodded. ''Well, I came back out a few minutes later to try to find you. You know, after what you'd said finally sank in. But of course you were gone.''

She grinned with the memory of her own behavior after she'd left the restaurant. ''While we're at it, I've got a little confession of my own.'' He looked at her in surprise. ''I came back to that restaurant a little while later, but you were gone, too.''

''You're kidding! Why?''

''Why?'' she asked in surprise. ''I was mad. If you remember, you did accuse me of trying to rip you off. For a hundred bucks? Isn't that what you said?'' He nodded sheepishly. ''So I was going to set you straight.''

''I may have gotten a little carried away,'' he admitted.

She nodded at the memory. ''As I recall, you threatened to call the police.''

''I guess I did, didn't I? Well, you'd just impugned my poor grandfather's good name,'' he said with the hint of a smile.

''I swear I thought you were digging around about him for the same reason I was. How was I supposed to know he was your grandfather?''

''I know, I know. But as you've certainly figured out by now, I know next to nothing about my grandfather, whether he ever had a good name to protect or not. But the fact is whenever you hear someone say something bad about a family member your natural reaction is to fight back.'' He laughed. ''By the way, I just learned the truth in those little words of wisdom yesterday. I couldn't believe it myself that I got so bent out of shape when you said what you said about a man I'd never even laid eyes on. Blood is thicker than water. Isn't that what that little expression is supposed to mean? I guess you took me by surprise. I'll blame it on that, anyway.'' He cocked his head and looked at her in an inquisitive way. ''This is crazy. You know as much about my grandfather as I do, more maybe, and I don't even know your name.'' He held out his hand. ''I'm Graham Stahmers.''

That was one question of hers answered. He didn't carry the LeClaire name. She took the proffered hand, strong and firm, and they shook. ''And I'm Ellie Regan.''

''Well, Ellie Regan,'' he said, ''so you came to Wyoming just to hunt down my grandfather?''

Fifteen minutes ago such words might have set her off, but she was beginning to understand this man's sense of humor. A certain tone in his voice, but also something he did with an eyebrow let her know he was poking fun. Two could play that game. ''I was hoping by now I'd be pumping oil out of my own well.''

He laughed. ''So sorry your dreams couldn't come true.'' From the sound in his voice Ellie decided he might have been talking about his own dreams as much as her own. ''So where are you from?''

''Dubuque, Iowa,'' she responded.

''Really? We're practically neighbors. I'm from Chicago.''

''Chicago! I grew up in Bloomington,'' she informed him, struck by the continuing coincidences surrounding their meeting. ''We used to go into the city all the time. Especially in the summer to see the Sox play.''

There was that smile again. ''The White Sox? Do they still play baseball?''

''Oh, no!'' she moaned in an exaggerated voice. ''You're not a Cubs fan?''

''Is there another team?''

''Then you have my sympathy,'' she said with mock solemnity. ''What are they? Ten games out? But it's still early in the season, though. Right?''

He laughed. ''I don't think either one of us has all that much to brag about. It's barely June and they're both practically out of the race.''

''The Sox have got two starting pitchers out with injuries,'' she said defensively. ''They'll be back in the thick of things by the middle of June.''

"Uh-huh," he said in a tone that suggested how unconvinced he really was. "Of course by then they'll be too far out to catch up." She offered no further argument to his prophesy, knowing that he was probably right. He studied her with that twinkle in his eyes. "Just my luck. I meet a beautiful woman on vacation and not only does she bad-mouth my poor, dead grandfather but she's got to be a Sox fan."

Ellie could feel the blush rise to her cheeks when he called her beautiful, and she only hoped the sun she'd taken on her hike the day before would offer some camouflage. "Sorry," she said.

"Are you on vacation out here, or did you come out for the express purpose of claiming your oil well?"

"The oil well thing was just for fun. I've always wanted to see this area, especially the Black Hills, so I decided to do some investigating at the same time."

"And you're traveling by yourself?" He tried to make the question sound offhand, but it didn't come out quite that way.

"I tried to talk my roommate into coming along, but she's getting married this fall and begged off because she says she has too much to do."

"Ah," he said with a thoughtful nod of the head. He let his gaze rest on her face. He hadn't been talking just to hear himself talk when he'd called her a beautiful woman moments earlier. She *was* beautiful. He'd decided that yesterday after the confrontation at the restaurant. Was that the reason he'd left his table to look for her in the street? It might have had something to do with it, though hearing her mention his own grandfather's name nearly dropped him in his tracks. He watched her eyes—so expressive. He knew he'd embarrassed her when he said she was beautiful. He could tell by the flush that tried to show on her cheeks. Her skin was so perfectly tanned it had been hard to tell. He tried to remember her hair, hidden today by her safari hat. It was dark, he knew that, and short but kind of wavy all over. He decided that was probably not the way a woman would care to have her hair described, but it was the best he could do. That was what he could recall. She was tall and slender. He tried to remember her height in relation to his his tall frame as they stood on the street. He'd guess she was about five-foot-eight. He was suddenly aware of that raised left eyebrow she seemed to use to express herself and realized she'd caught him staring. Now it was his turn to hide embarrassment by clasping his arms across his chest to keep his fingertips from doing their usual nervous tapping against each other or anything else that happened to be handy. He'd learned long ago that he could keep them in check with the arm-clasping routine, but he didn't know the action made him look so unapproachable. ''So, what do you do back there in Dubuque?''

She was secretly enjoying his discomfort. He'd been a little too confident to suit her. ''I'm a high school guidance counselor.''

''Oh, really? So you have a nice long vacation for travel?''

She disliked the reference to long vacation time, since she found that college work and conferences had a way of gobbling up much of that free time. ''I'm afraid I don't have much time to travel. I'm trying to get an advanced degree and the only time I can take courses is during the summer.''

He detected an ever-so-slight chill in her voice and realized he'd said the wrong thing. Again. ''Of course. So, how do you like working with teenagers?''

Ellie struggled to keep the look of irritation off her face. Why was it people insist on talking about teenagers as if they were lepers? she wondered, not for the first time. ''I like it fine. Naturally, as with all *human beings,* there are some bad ones but also a lot of good ones.'' She thought she might have emphasized ''human beings'' a little more than she needed, but he had it coming. ''So what about you? What's your line of work?''

''I'm a travel writer.''

She was interested. ''Really! Do you work for a specific magazine?''

''I freelance quite a bit, but I take assignments on occasion. And I've done a few television scripts—you know, for the travel channels. But that's not my favorite thing. You've got too many people involved. Right now I'm pitching an idea for a book on covering the country from one end to the other at bed-and-breakfasts, but so far no takers.''

''What a great idea!''

''Do you think so? I like it, too, but we must be the only ones.''

She frowned. ''I don't understand that. With the popularity of B-and-Bs? It seems like an automatic.''

He was pleased with her interest. ''I'm glad you think so. I think the sticking point is that I want enough advance to cover the time it will take to actually research the B-and-Bs. Publishers want me to hand them the finished book, but I can't afford to do that.''

She nodded. ''So, are you working on something right now?''

''Sure am.'' He held out his hands as if introducing her to the area around them. ''Welcome to my office.'' He patted his camera case. ''I've got my trusty camera and a notepad. That's all I need. Except for my laptop back at the motel.''

''That sounds so exciting.''

''If you like to travel. Which I do.''

''So do I, but I don't get to do much of it. I went to Europe during my junior year in college, and I'm dying to go back. Do you travel out of the country?''

''Quite a bit. I try to do that on assignment so my expenses are covered.''

''That sounds like so much fun. You get to go to all the places you want, and all you have to do is write about it.''

He shot her a look. ''Well, it isn't all a bed of roses, you know. Sometimes I have to go places I don't really want to go to. Then there's the travel part. Sitting in airports, trying to arrange transportation, flying in nasty weather. It's not all a picnic.''

''I suppose not,'' she agreed, remembering her own irritation at his assumption that her summer was her own to do with as she pleased. She glanced up at the strange shaft of rock looming up at them through the trees across the road. ''So, you're doing an article on Devils Tower?''

He followed where she was looking up the side of the rocky

formation. "Actually I'm doing a couple of pieces on it. I'm doing something for the *Tribune's* Sunday magazine that should run sometime in the middle of July, and then I'm doing a longer article for *Modern Maturity* about this"—he nodded toward the tower—"and the whole Black Hills thing. You know, Mount Rushmore and the Crazy Horse monument and some of the caves. That won't be published until next April or May, just before the summer vacation season. Then I'm doing a separate article about the Crazy Horse carving. *The New Yorker* is interested, but that's not a sure sale. That won't be your typical travel piece. I'm going to profile the widow of the sculptor who started the whole thing. She's been the strength behind it since he died. I have an appointment with her day after tomorrow."

He turned back toward Ellie and she saw in his eyes the excitement for what he was doing. "*The New Yorker*. That *would* be something."

"They took one of my pieces a while back. I guess it's been about four years. Another one would definitely be more than okay, I can tell you."

"How about ghost towns? Any interest there?" she asked. "I visited one yesterday."

His eyes widened. "Sure. Where? Ghost towns always make good copy."

"It's not far away."

"Maybe you could show me," he said as he watched her eyes.

"I suppose I could. I was planning to work my way back to Rapid City today, but there's no hurry."

"Great." He took his hat off and scared away a honeybee investigating his left knee. "So does that mean you've given up on the oil business? Your stock is worthless?"

"Oh, I assume so. Didn't they tell you at the museum that your grandfather sold out or was bought out?"

"Yes, and I wasn't even looking for that. I wanted anything they had on LeClaire, and that's what they gave me."

Ellie was becoming more at ease in the company of this man, but the wooden bench the two were sitting on was another matter. Its rough surface and awkward design seemed to defy every attempt she made to find a comfortable position. She shifted awkwardly in her place, pulling one heel up to support herself. He noticed her discomfort. "Were you getting ready to take the hike?" She nodded. "Me, too. Want to join forces? That is, if you don't mind a slow trip. I need to take some pictures and make a few notes."

"Sounds good to me," she answered eagerly. "It isn't every day I get a chance to watch a famous writer at work."

He threw her a look. "You're making fun. I've been talking about myself too much, haven't I?"

She was concerned that he had misconstrued her meaning. "No, really, I mean it. I wasn't making fun. I'm always looking for information on professions that I can tell our students about."

"Oh," he said simply, quite satisfied with her explanation. "Shall we see what this big rock is all about?" he asked with a nod toward the tower. He stood and began extracting his camera from its carrying case, checking the settings, and readying it for service. Ellie shrugged into her backpack, and the two made their way back across the road toward the trailhead. Looking about her, Ellie could see the stream of brightly dressed tourists flocking from the parking lot toward the visitor center. As they moved into the trees, she spotted a handful of youngsters jumping from boulder to boulder among the piles of rock at the base of the tower. That, in spite of a sign she'd just passed on the trail warning of the possibility of rattlesnakes. "I guess Lil was right," she said.

Graham was walking ahead of her on the narrow path. He stopped and swung around to face her. "What's that?"

"I said Lil was right. She's a desk clerk at the motel where I'm staying. She says the best time to visit here is early morning, and now I know what she was talking about. She says it gets too crowded later in the day, and if this is any indication, she wasn't kidding."

It took them nearly an hour and a half to make the circuit of the tower, scarcely over a mile in length and most of that flat, but Ellie discovered Graham hadn't been kidding when he warned of a slow walk. They stopped often for him to take pictures and jot notes in a steno-type notebook he kept in a front pocket of the camera case. She'd never seen anyone take so many pictures of one thing. He'd snap off four or five shots of one scene, adjusting the camera settings before each shot. She saw him load the camera twice but wasn't certain if the film was twenty-four exposure or thirty-six. At one point he climbed a pile of rock rubble for a particular camera angle, and she called to him about the sign she'd seen warning of rattlesnakes.

"They're just little prairie rattlers," he said with a grin. "They can't jump very high." He pointed to his sturdy hiking boots which came only part way up his ankle. For her money that seemed to leave a lot of exposed skin that any self-respecting rattlesnake, even a little prairie rattler as he called them, would love to sink his fangs into. When he climbed down after snapping off five or six shots, he turned to her. "Did you check out the displays in the visitor center?"

"A couple," she answered.

"Did you see the one about the snakes?"

"No," she said. "Snakes and I are not on the best of terms."

"So I gathered," he said with that smile of his. "Well, anyway, from what I read, they find rattlers on top of this thing." He nodded at the tower. "Can you believe it? They climb all the way to the top. Climbers on the way up have reported coming face-to-face with rattlers sunning themselves on ledges. How would you like to poke your nose over a rock while you're hanging in space and say hello to Mr. Rattlesnake?"

Ellie shivered at the thought. "No, thank you. I have no intention of coming anywhere near face-to-face with any snake, let alone one that has fangs and rattles."

He laughed. He couldn't resist teasing. "They're probably all around us." He waved a hand at the piles of rocks around them. "They live in those rocks, you know."

"Stop it!" she shouted as she jumped toward the center of the trail and away from the rocks that bordered it.

He laughed again. "Come on now. Remember, they're more afraid of you than you are of them."

"I find that highly doubtful," Ellie said.

"What do you mean?"

"I just mean that it's not possible they could be more frightened of me than I am of them."

Graham came to the obvious conclusion at that moment that her fear of snakes was definitely not something to be trifled with. At least not out here where there was a real possibility of seeing one of the creatures. "Well, you've got me there. I have no way of measuring your fear against that of a snake. So suppose we just call it a draw."

She nodded. "Sounds good to me."

He swung around and continued along the trail, stopping thirty feet further to analyze a spectacular view of the distant countryside for the proper camera angle and setting. He took several shots.

"I didn't know writers took so many pictures," Ellie observed.

"Travel writers do," he said as he advanced the film and slipped the lens cap in place. "Sometimes I can sell my photos when I sell the article. But even if I can't, they still help jog my memory when I'm writing."

"Hmm."

"Do you know where all this rock came from?" He was looking at the piles of broken rock littering the base of the tower.

"It fell off the side," she said as she looked up at the long grooves running down the side of the tower, thinking again of the legend of the bear claw marks.

"Do you know when the last chunk fell off?"

She gave the tower an appraising glance and then looked at the piles of rock rubble around them. "Probably not too long ago," she said. "I'd say maybe twenty or thirty years."

"Ten thousand years ago," he announced with a satisfied look, confident that the news would take her by surprise. And he wasn't disappointed in her reaction.

"Ten thousand years!" she practically shouted.

"That's what geologists claim."

"That seems pretty hard to believe."

"All I'm telling you is what I read."

"I wasn't doubting you. Just geologists."

He looked around him. "It does seem pretty wild, doesn't it? What I'd like to know is, how do they figure out things like that?"

She looked up again. "I hope some of those chunks up there don't decide it's about time to make modern history."

"Just think, we could be part of a geologic moment."

"Thanks anyway, but I think I'll pass on that opportunity."

"Me, too," he agreed with a grin as he turned to set off once again.

Ellie enjoyed the hike. The oddity of this geological formation poking up out of the ground in the midst of a nearly flat countryside was enough to hold her attention all by itself. And the beauty of the green fields stretching for miles in all directions was breathtaking. But she had to admit her main fascination was with Mr. Graham Stahmers. She was amused at his inquisitiveness about everything. He was almost like a little boy in his need to explore. She guessed such a trait must be a great advantage to a writer whose intention was to interest a reader in something he was visiting. She found his gawking contagious. Fresh into the hike he'd spotted an Indian prayer bundle. A small sign near the trailhead requested respect for the religious symbols, but Ellie doubted she would have even seen one on her own. Then it was two climbers struggling to scale the rocky cliff. They were high above the trail, but his keen eyes made out the bright clothing they were wearing. Now, she looked up as he pointed to birds circling lazily at the top of the tower. "Turkey vultures," he reported.

"How do you know that?"

"I'm pretty sure that's what they are. They look like turkey vultures. They're trying to nail rabbits or gophers or something like that in the rocks."

"Or snakes?" she asked hopefully.

He laughed. "I don't know if those little delicacies are a part of their menu or not."

They rounded a final bend in the trail and could see the visitor center through the trees. Graham checked his watch, and Ellie, seeing him do so, did the same. It was nearly 11:30. "I'm starved," he said. "Do they serve food over there?" He nodded toward the log structure.

"Snacks and such. I've got a cheese sandwich and chips in my backpack. If we picked up a few things there, we'd have plenty for a picnic. Want to share?"

He stared. "You mean you had food in there all this time?"

"Of course. I never go anywhere without plenty to eat," she said with a grin. "All you had to do was ask. I would think a travel writer would know enough to bring along something to eat on a hike."

He nodded in agreement. "I know. But I wasn't hungry when I left this morning." He laughed at how foolish that sounded. "I guess that's kind of a stupid excuse, isn't it?"

They picked up a few things at the snack shop, including something to drink, and found an unoccupied log picnic table beneath a tall lodgepole pine. Ellie divided her sandwich, and the two dug in, relishing their little meal after the refreshing hike. She tossed her safari hat on the table and ran a hand through her dark hair. "So, Mr. Travel Writer," she said with a tilt of her head, "are you going to give Devils Tower a good review?"

Graham had just taken a bite of sandwich, and all he could do was nod his head in the affirmative. He swallowed and washed the bite down with a long drink from his can of soda. "Definitely," he finally managed. "It's beautiful. Anyone who comes within a hundred miles of here has got to make the side trip. Don't you agree?"

Ellie nodded. "I'm glad I came, that's for sure." She stared up at the tower. "It has kind of mystical aura about it. I can definitely understand why it's sacred to Native Americans."

Ellie lowered her eyes from a survey of the tower to find Graham studying her intently. "Will you have dinner with me tonight?" he asked suddenly.

"Tonight? I—I don't know if I can."

"You've got to let me pay you back for this sandwich,"

he added quickly, raising what little remained of the cheese on rye.

''You don't have to do that,'' she said with a smile.

''Maybe not, but I want to.''

''I was planning to go to Rapid City today after I left here. In fact, I already checked out of my motel.''

''I found an excellent restaurant I know you'd like,'' he continued, undaunted.

''Well . . .''

He could hear a hesitation in her tone and he pressed his advantage. ''Besides, you promised you'd show me that ghost town.''

''Well, I guess I could stay another night. I don't have any particular schedule.''

''Good,'' he said. ''It's settled. Where can I pick you up?''

She laughed. ''I was staying at the Pine Rest Motel. I guess I can get in there again. They weren't all that busy. It's just west of the main part of town. Right across the street from some kind of lumber mill or something. There are stacks and stacks of fresh-cut boards inside a big chainlink fence.''

''I'm pretty sure I drove past that on my first day in town. I can find it. How does six-thirty sound?''

''That would be fine.''

''Good. I'll be there.'' He polished off the last of his sandwich and smiled to himself, happy that a grandfather he'd never known had made a trip across Iowa some sixty years ago, even if his intentions had been less than honorable.

Chapter Five

Ellie parked her car in front of the office and went inside, trying desperately to hide her sheepish look from Lil who was at her usual daytime place behind the counter. The woman glanced up from a magazine, and her face registered surprise. "Thought you'd be in Rapid City by now."

"Change of plan. Is my old room still available?"

The woman stood and scrutinized her checkin list. She glanced up. "You were in eleven?"

"I think that was it," Ellie responded.

Lil hesitated, looking closer at the sheet. "Uh, nope, that's taken, but I can put ya in twelve. That all right?"

"Sure."

The woman extracted a sign-in card from a box under the counter and slapped it, along with a pen, in front of Ellie. She lounged against the counter, propping her jaw on an open palm as she watched the sign-in process. "So how was it up to Devils Tower?"

Ellie glanced up from her chore. "Oh, it was great. You were right about going early. But Graham and I had already done the hike before it got really crowded." Her cheeks reddened when she realized she'd said more than she intended. She could only hope Lil hadn't caught the reference to Graham, and then she felt foolish for even caring. It wasn't as if she were facing an interrogation from her mother, she reminded herself as she scribbled furiously at the sign-in card without looking up.

But if Ellie had bothered to notice, she would have seen the tired, gray eyes across the counter from her suddenly come to life. There was nothing wrong with the woman's hearing *or* her curiosity. She straightened from her slouch. "Did ya join, some tour up there I don't know about? I could have sworn I heard ya say somethin' 'bout somebody called Graham just now."

"I met someone and we hiked the trail," Ellie said, trying to make her voice sound casual as she filled in her car license information. "It's no big deal."

"Come now, young lady. You're not goin' to leave old Lil hangin' just like that, are ya? I'm an old woman, and this here's a boring town." She grinned. "Besides, I'm tired of watchin' the television."

The words "young lady" brought a smile to Ellie's face as she thought of her mother. *Maybe this* is *going to be an interrogation,* she decided. *Well, it's my own fault. I could have gone to some other motel.* But secretly she was glad she hadn't. She needed to tell someone all that had happened, and Lil seemed a more than adequate listener. Ellie had felt a strange kinship with the woman from the first moment she'd met her. She reminded her for all the world of Great-aunt Rose on her father's side, long dead now. Rose visited at Christmas every year until she died when Ellie was ten. Ellie kept her distance from the wrinkled woman at first until she found out just how sweet and loving she really was. Ellie would always be grateful to Aunt Rose for erasing forever any stigma for her in the word "old." Aunt Rose might have looked old, but she acted anything but. Like when she played Crazy Eights at the kitchen table or when she crawled under a card table house covered with a blanket to sip tea at a doll party or when she snagged icicles from the porch eaves for the two of them to suck on. Ellie remembered her shock when she read the prayer card for Aunt Rose's funeral to discover the woman was eighty-eight when she died.

Ellie wasn't sure what there was about Lil that reminded

her of Aunt Rose. It was a lot of little things. She certainly
wasn't nearly as old as Aunt Rose, but snow-white hair and
a fair share of wrinkles would earn her a senior citizen dis-
count with no questions asked. She had more than a touch of
an Irish brogue that hinted at Aunt Rose's much thicker ac-
cent. They both had a way of raising an eyebrow or widening
their eyes to effect. Sometimes the look said it all; sometimes
it merely added punctuation. Ellie had been told more than
once she had the same trait, but she was sure family members
who told her so were exaggerating. For whatever reasons, the
woman behind the counter reminded her of dear Aunt Rose.
So she told all to a stranger who really wasn't a stranger, and
Lil was the good listener she knew she would be, reacting
with surprise and shock at all the right places. She told about
the stranger who preceded her at every step in her search for
the elusive oil well. She told about confronting this same man
outside the restaurant and then the improbability of running
into him again at Devils Tower.

"You're not joshin' old Lil now!" the woman said at the
Devils Tower news, her eyes round with surprise.

"I know. It sounds like some science fiction movie, doesn't
it? But there I was, standing in front of him as he was trying
to take a picture."

"And you say this fella, Graham you called him, he's the
grandson of the scoundrel what robbed your poor old
grandfather?"

"That's right. Graham Stahmers is his name. But there's
no way of knowing for sure if his grandfather intended to steal
the money from Grandpa."

Lil received this new information with a dubious arch of
both eyebrows that added fresh wrinkles to an already wrinkled forehead. She appreciated simple explanations for things,
especially the character of people. She was quick to judge and
slow to change an opinion once she'd made it. That was why
she'd never held much stock in the notion of rehabilitation.
"Ya don't make a rotten apple taste good by talkin' at it,"
she was fond of saying. "Hmm," she said now in a tone that
suggested the illegal intention of Graham Stahmers' grandfa-

ther over sixty years ago was a matter not worthy of discussion. A quizzical look crossed her face as a new thought struck her. "That's not the name of the old fella you're lookin' for, the one what signed your oil thingamajig."

"No, that's LeClaire," Ellie volunteered. "His mother was a LeClaire."

"And I suppose he's out here huntin' for lost oil wells, too?" the other woman said more than asked.

"I don't think so. It sounds like he's trying to trace his family." As she answered Lil's question, Ellie realized how little she really knew about Graham's own reason for being here. He'd mentioned his mother, and he'd appeared anxious to learn anything he could about his grandfather. She realized, thanks to Lil, she had some questions of her own that needed asking.

Lil sighed. "Well, I'll be," she said, genuinely impressed with the story. "Ya got more than ya bargained for in your little treasure hunt, didn't ya?" She cocked an eyebrow. "Is he a cute one?"

"Well, yes," Ellie said hesitantly. "But it's nothing like that."

"Oh, 'course not," Lil said in a tone that suggested she didn't believe a word of it. "Not from around here, I guess?"

"No, Chicago."

"Oh," she said, obviously disappointed at that news and making little attempt to hide her disdain for the big city. "And I suppose he's one of them lawyers." To Lil a city and a lawyer seemed a perfect fit.

"No, he's a travel writer."

"Ya don't say?" She was at least mildly interested again.

"In fact, he's writing an article about this whole area. I told him I'd take him to see Maryville."

"Oh, did ya now?" Lil allowed herself to imagine her name in print. "And did ya tell him I told ya about the place?"

Ellie's lips quivered ever so slightly as she struggled to keep from smiling. "Yes, I believe I did. If I didn't, I'll mention it tonight."

"Tonight, ya say?"

"He's taking me to dinner."

"He's not lettin' the grass grow under his feet, is he?"

Ellie sighed and shook her head in an attempt to let Lil know she had the wrong impression about dinner. "We just have some more things to talk about."

"Uh-huh." There was that tone again. "And is this Graham fella married?"

The direct question took Ellie so much by surprise that she answered too quickly. "No." Then seeing Lil's smile, her face reddened all over again. "I mean, I don't think he is. At least he wasn't wearing a ring." She had said too much as usual.

"But ya were looking for a ring, were ya now?"

Ellie knew it was useless to try to explain how she had noticed such a thing. Lil wouldn't believe her anyway. She had her gang of friends back home to blame. During college days they had made a joke of checking for a wedding band when any eligible male came within thirty feet. It became a kind of game. Who would be first to spot the presence or absence of a shiny band on the ring finger? She still did it, out of habit. She guessed she'd still be doing it even after twenty-five years of blissful marriage. But telling all that to Lil would be a waste of breath. "I always notice things like that," she said. "It doesn't mean anything."

" 'Course not," Lil said in the voice that Ellie was becoming quite familiar with, the one that meant just the opposite of what she was saying. "Mind my words now. The apple never falls far from the tree."

Ellie went out the door mulling over that last bit of advice. She wondered if Lil knew herself the meanings of the aphorisms she was so fond of repeating. She dragged her suitcases out of the trunk of the car and lugged them into her new room. She had three hours to kill before dinner, and she decided to spend part of that time at a pottery factory she'd passed on the way back into town today. She needed to pick up some gifts for friends back home.

Ellie heard a car door slam and slid aside the heavy drape covering the window of her room just in time to see Graham standing by his car, scanning the row of doors before him. *Of course,* she realized, *he has no idea which room is mine or even if I was able to get back in at Pine Rest. We didn't even plan for such a possibility,* she remembered, feeling just a little foolish. She hurriedly unlocked her door and tugged it open, but not before he had made up his mind to solicit help at the front office. "I'm here," she called.

He spun around at the sound of her voice, obviously relieved. "Oh, good. I didn't think until I pulled in that you might not have gotten your room back."

She stepped out and closed the door behind her. "Actually, I didn't. Not the same one anyway, but they had another vacancy." She examined him as he walked toward her. *It's no wonder he had the courthouse and the museum in such a flurry,* she thought. He was wearing gray slacks, a pale blue sports shirt, and a dark blue blazer. His light brown hair, hidden beneath his safari hat in the morning, she noticed was full and wavy.

He smiled as he came closer. "We didn't plan very well, did we? What were you going to do if you couldn't get back in here?"

"As a matter of fact, I just figured that out as I came out the door. I would have driven back here a little before six-thirty and waited for you in the parking lot."

"Very good!" he said, obviously impressed. "I'm not certain I would have thought of that." He nodded toward his car. "Shall we?" He gave her an admiring glance as he held the door. She was wearing a pair of dark slacks and a simple white blouse, but to him she couldn't have looked more beautiful. If only he knew the dither she'd been in after her shower about what to wear. As it turned out, she counted herself lucky to be living out of a suitcase, because her clothes options weren't really all that great. She blamed her indecision on the fact that she was clueless about what type of restaurant they would be going to.

The restaurant Graham had spotted and even tried himself the previous night was called Mountain View though he wasn't quite certain about the name since all he could see from the floor-to-ceiling windows was the rolling grasslands to the west and the outlines of the Black Hills to the east. He knew it would take a strong telescope to see the real mountains west and southwest of here—the Medicine Bow Range, Deer Creek, and, of course, the Bighorns. He related these thoughts to Ellie when they were comfortably seated near a window on the Black Hills side. She was studying the rough interior around them as he talked. She liked the feel of the place. There were heavy beams and wide-open spaces and a huge stone fireplace, unnecessary at this time of year, to be sure, but she knew it would add to the coziness in the fall and winter. Her only objection was with the mounted animal heads adorning the walls—buffalo, mountain sheep, deer, elk. She knew it was a taste thing, but she would enjoy her dinner more without these poor creatures looking over her shoulder.

"I think you're being too picky," she said in answer to his thing about the name. "We know the mountains are out there even if we can't see them."

"But that's just the point." He was discovering it was fun to tease her. She never let anything just lie there. She would have some answer. "It says 'view,' " he went on, a hint of a smile on his lips. "Doesn't that mean we should be able to *see* mountains? You wouldn't have a restaurant in Dubuque called Mountain View, would you?"

"For all I know there probably is one," she said with a laugh. She turned to stare out the window near them. "Just look out there. Don't those look like mountains?"

She could see he was set to disagree. "I know, I know, technically they're hills, but they look like mountains, don't they? Especially from this far away. Anyway," she added as an afterthought, "you wouldn't want to call a place Hill View. That just doesn't sound right."

"But how about Black Hills View?" he said suddenly, and they both laughed.

"Hey, that's not bad," she said. "I wonder why they didn't think of that? You travel writers just have a way with words." The waiter approached the table at that moment and Ellie, still in a joking mood, pointed a finger across at Graham. "He has a bone to pick about your name."

The surprised teenager glanced down at the nametag pinned to his shirt. "Eldridge is my grandfather's name," he said in a voice mixed with hurt and anger.

Graham buried his face in his napkin to try to hold in his laughter, but Ellie controlled herself with tremendous effort. "No, not *your* name. Eldridge is a perfectly fine name. I was talking about the name of the restaurant." She looked across at Graham just then and wished she hadn't because all she could see of him was from the eyes up. The rest of his face was covered with a burgundy napkin. His eyes were watering from the struggle he was having. "My friend here, who seems to be choking just now, thinks the name of the restaurant should be changed to Black Hills View." She was met with a blank look from Eldridge.

"I'll tell my boss," he said.

"That won't be necessary," she assured him. "We were just kidding." They took the menus he offered and each ordered a glass of wine before the young man retreated to the kitchen. Ellie watched him go. "Eldridge isn't exactly a man of the world yet, is he? I hope he laughs about our little exchange later when he figures it out."

Graham was wiping the tears from his eyes. "I am impressed. How did you do that? Keep a straight face, I mean?"

"Professional discipline," she confided to him with a smug look. "Kids tell me some strange things, I can tell you, and if I so much as smile at them, let alone laugh out loud, they'd dissolve on the spot into an embarrassed puddle. I suppose you don't remember saying something stupid like that when you were his age?"

He laughed at the idea. "I probably was too stupid to know I was saying something stupid." A sudden thought struck him. "No, I *do* remember one." He smiled when he remembered the time.

"Well? Out with it."

"I used to play the clarinet when I was a kid. We had a new band man at school, and when I went in for my first lesson, he says to me, 'So, what's your handle?' I held up my clarinet and said, 'Clarinet.' ''

Ellie giggled. ''That *was* pretty stupid.''

''Well, how was I supposed to know he wanted to know my name?''

''So, what did he say?''

''I don't remember. I didn't figure out I'd said anything weird until I told my folks that night at dinner. They just about laughed me out of the house. They didn't have your—what did you call it, profession discipline? But Mr. McTaggert was cool about it.'' Her look was quizzical. ''He was the band man. He was a cool guy anyway.''

She nodded. ''And this cool guy obviously had professional discipline. The poor fellow was probably popping blood vessels in his brain trying to keep all that in.'' Just then the bartender appeared with their wine, and close on his heels Eldridge was back for their orders. They were both very formal with him this time, but Ellie noticed that he kept sneaking peeks at each of them in turn over his order pad as if he were waiting for what they might do next. When he was gone, Ellie took a sip of her white wine. ''I didn't think to ask. What did you find out at Lassiter Petroleum yesterday?''

He raised an eyebrow. ''Still thinking about that oil well?''

''No!'' She was mildly indignant. ''I was thinking about your grandfather, if you must know.''

''Oh.'' His tone was contrite for his accusing question. ''Well, I didn't find out much about him, but there was a record that Lassiter acquired Whitiker Oil in 1945. I already knew that from the museum, though. I suppose they told you that, didn't they?'' Ellie nodded. ''The folks at Lassiter didn't know anything about any LeClaire, though,'' he added.

Ellie pursed her lips in thought. ''Hmm.'' She finally decided to ask the question that had been on her mind all afternoon. ''Why are you so interested in finding out about your grandfather after all these years?''

''It's a long story.'' His tone and manner both suggested it would remain untold if he had his way.

She had no intention of letting him off the hook so easily.

She made her living drawing important life stories out of teenagers, and she was certain she could do it with him. She had always believed that talking about a problem was the first step toward doing something about it. "You mentioned your mother. Did she ask you to check on her dad?"

"No," he said quickly. "She doesn't have a clue I'm doing this."

"Would she mind if she knew you were out here?"

"Probably. Oh, maybe not. I just don't know."

Ellie was cradling her wineglass in the hollow of her left hand. She studied Graham across the table. She thought it strange he hadn't told his mother what he was doing, and she could tell talking about it was making him uncomfortable. "She's buried her childhood?"

"Something like that. More like she never had a childhood to bury. She can't remember much of it, anyway. She spent something like seven years in an orphanage in Sioux Falls, South Dakota."

Eldridge picked a bad time to arrive with their salads. Ellie waited until he was gone before prompting Graham for more of the story. "What year was that? I mean when she went to the orphanage."

"1942, she thinks."

"And how old would she have been then?"

"If it *was* 1942, she would have been five. She's kind of foggy about that time, and the orphanage is closed now so there aren't any records. I checked before I came out here. But anyway she thinks that's about how old she was."

"Did her parents die? Is that why she went to the orphanage?"

Graham shrugged his shoulders. "I don't know. *She* doesn't know," he added quickly when he saw her questioning look. "I know that sounds crazy, but she doesn't. She thinks they were alive. She remembers her mother kissing her good-bye, but then she's not even sure about that. Sometimes she thinks she may have dreamed it. She has a vague memory of seeing someone in bed—sick or injured or something. She thinks it was her father. I'm not clear on all of this myself because she only talked to me about it once, and that was two years ago. She'd had cancer surgery, and we talked in the hospital. I don't think she thought she was going to make it."

"How is she now?" Ellie asked, her eyes expressing her concern.

"Not great. She had to have surgery again last fall for a reoccurrence, and then she had pneumonia in February, so all in all it hasn't been a good year."

"I'm so sorry." She added a touch more dressing to her salad. "So what happened with the orphanage? Was she adopted?"

He looked up from his salad. "Finally. She was twelve. A couple from Pipestone, Minnesota, adopted her. They were the only grandparents I've ever known. My dad's folks were both dead by the time I came along."

"Hmm," she said. Something was bothering her. "Hasn't your mom ever wanted to come back here on her own to find out what happened to her folks?"

"I don't think so. I think she's convinced they abandoned her. Like I said, she's only talked about it with me that one time. I think she's still pretty bitter."

"She didn't have any brothers or sisters?"

He shook his head. "Who knows? She told me she thinks she remembers a baby, but it's like the thing with her mother. It's probably a dream."

Eldridge arrived laden with a heavy tray. They both set their unfinished salads aside to make room for the main entree. The inexperienced waiter awkwardly situated the hot plates containing Ellie's Jerusalem chicken and Graham's medium-rare steak in front of the pair before moving away. Graham looked over at her before he started on his steak. "So now you know the whole sordid past of the LeClaire family. Not only was my grandfather a cheat, as you have pointed out so clearly, but he was a deadbeat who couldn't even keep his family together."

Ellie didn't like his tone. "You don't know that for sure."

"The heck I don't. Look at what happened to my mother. How much more proof do you need?"

Ellie was feeling increasingly uncomfortable. She concentrated on her chicken, finding it difficult to swallow the bites even though the dish was tasty. The sound of their forks and knives scraping against the plates seemed loud in her ears. She wanted this dinner to be over. *Why did I agree to come?* she asked herself. *Better yet, why did I have to meddle? He made it perfectly clear he didn't want to talk about his mother, but did I listen? No, of course not.* Still, it wasn't in her nature to give up quite so easily. And as the two continued their meal in the awkward silence, new questions popped into her head. Finally she set down her fork and looked across the table at him. "What did you expect to find when you came out here, anyway? You laugh at me because I was looking for an oil well. What were *you* looking for?"

His eyes had taken on almost a fierceness as they met hers. "What was I looking for? I'll tell you what I was looking for. I was hoping I could find some reason why a mother and father would give up a little girl to live a life in an orphanage. That's what I was looking for." He went back to his steak, and the intensity with which he attacked the next bite with knife and fork left little doubt as to his state of mind.

Ellie, a firm believer that relief often follows getting things out in the open, didn't let up. "And just what have you found out about your grandfather since you've been here?"

"As I said no more than two minutes ago, I found out he was a cheat who robbed people of their hard-earned money with no intention of paying it back." He pointed his fork at her. "And I learned that from you."

"You have a one-track mind, Mr. Stahmers."

"Oh, is that so?"

"Yes, that's so. What do you really know? You have one example in which your grandfather took a thousand dollars from my grandfather, who, by the way, gave it to him willingly, in exchange for shares of stock in an oil company which we now know your grandfather at one time owned. That was big news to me, I can tell you. When I came out here, I was pretty sure I'd find there never was an oil company. That he'd made it up as a way of stealing money. In fact, I had strong

doubts that there was even a man by the name of Jerome
LeClaire. I thought he'd made that up, too. But don't you see?
There *was* a company. So how do we know what was going
on inside his head, what his intentions were? Isn't it just possible he hoped to be able to pay back big dividends on that
money?''

Graham shook his head and gave a little forced laugh.
''Why do you insist on defending him? You sound like you're
pleading his case in court. And you were the one who came
up to me in the street and told me to my face that my grandfather was a cheat.''

''I didn't know he was your grandfather at the time.''

''What does that have to do with anything? You still said
it. What could possibly have changed your mind?''

She shook her head. ''I don't know.'' She hesitated. ''It's . . .
it's a feeling I have. I'm positive there's still a lot we don't
know.''

''Women's intuition?'' He said it in a way that suggested
he strongly doubted the existence of such an instinct.

She looked up at him quickly, a fire in her eyes. ''Maybe
that's exactly what it is. Do you have a problem with that?''

He was surprised at her intensity, and he laughed a little
defensively. ''I guess not, not if you believe in it *that* much.''
They ate on in silence for a few minutes until finally he spoke
again. ''Listen, let's lighten up a little. Okay? We're supposed
to be celebrating our . . .'' His voice trailed off as if he were
thinking of what they should be celebrating. But the truth was
he'd intended to say ''our meeting'' but was suddenly reluctant to admit that their meeting, twice, as it turned out, and
by the most unbelievable of circumstances, was really so important to him. He settled for a reason to celebrate that he
knew would make her laugh. ''. . . hike around Devils Tower
without seeing a single rattlesnake.''

She was glad to laugh at that, to break the gloomy mood
they had gotten themselves into, though she wasn't satisfied
to leave so many unanswered questions just lying there. They
finished the meal cheerful enough though it was obvious the

two were picking their way around conversational minefields to avoid any repeat of their earlier flareup.

In the car on the way back into town, Ellie decided she had had it with all the denial. "I'm sorry if this offends you," she began, "but I just have to ask. You're not going to give up on trying to find out about your grandparents, are you? From what you told me, it sounds like the best thing for your mom right now would be to put her in touch with her past." She looked across at him behind the wheel, but his face was expressionless—or a better way to describe it was stony, she decided. When he said nothing, she rambled on: "There are still lots of things that could be done. You could check the courthouse again for death certificates and maybe birth certificates for any children. But your mom probably already has hers, I suppose." She looked at him again hopefully, but still nothing. She went on. "The woman at the museum said something about going through old newspapers Who knows where that might lead? Then there could be church records. One thing leads to another." She gave up on her monologue finally, was quiet for a few seconds, and then sighed loudly to show both her resignation and disgust. She glared across at him this time, not sure if she was more angry at his silence or his stubbornness.

"The answer is yes," he said suddenly.

"What?"

"I said the answer is yes."

"I heard what you said," she answered hotly. "I just don't know what you meant."

"You asked if I'm going to give up digging around in my grandparents' past, and I said yes."

She scowled. "I don't remember using the word 'digging around.' But anyway, why?"

"I already told you. My mother doesn't need to have it confirmed for her that her parents were deadbeats."

"And I keep telling you, you don't know that for sure."

"All signs point in that direction," he said doggedly.

"I swear," she said in a tone of total exasperation. "I've

known you for less than a day, and I can honestly say you're the most stubborn man I've ever met in my whole life.''

''At least I'll be remembered for something.''

She turned to stare out the window and was relieved to see the sign for Pine Rest not more than a block away. She had less than thirty seconds to endure the uncomfortable silence that had enveloped the pair. He pulled in behind her Toyota, and she opened the door and hopped out before the car had come to a full stop. ''I'm sorry,'' he said, but his words were lost in the loud slam of the door. ''Good-bye to you, too,'' he added as he swung the car around and made for the exit.

It was 8:00, and Ellie had slept poorly. She pushed open the door to the office and stumbled in wishing she could avoid Lil's inquiring eyes this morning, but knowing she hadn't signed her credit card voucher on checkin the day before. Lil glanced up from her magazine. ''Well, look what the cat drug in. What's wrong with you? Ya look awful.''

''Thanks so much,'' Ellie replied with a withering look.

Lil ignored the tone and the look. ''What? A late date?''

Another look. ''No.'' She attempted to ignore Lil's curiosity. ''I need to check out.''

Lil's eyes widened in surprise. ''What? Again? And so soon? What happened to Mr. Wonderful? And that fancy dinner of his?'' she added as an afterthought.

''Well,'' Ellie said, and frowned at the memory of last night. It wasn't the first time, since she had so unceremoniously slammed the car door in his face, that the memory had haunted her. She knew she had probably said too much, especially on the way back in the car. ''Meddled'' is the word her roommate would have used. But then again the man was stubborn and just plain impossible, hiding from his past like that. ''Let's just say we didn't see eye to eye on some things,'' she said by way of a simple explanation.

''Uh-huh,'' Lil replied knowingly. ''A little lovers' spat, was it?''

''Lil! You've been watching too many soaps. I barely knew the man. I certainly wouldn't call it a lovers' spat.''

As she had been conducting her inquisition, Lil had produced Ellie's credit card slip, totaled the amount, and slipped it across the counter for her to sign. "Don't talk to old Lil about men. Been down that road a time or two myself. They're a confusin' lot, purely confusin'."

Ellie was scratching her name on the credit card slip. "Well, you won't get any arguments from me on that score."

A new thought suddenly struck Lil. "What about the ghost town? Ya promised to take him." The dream about her name in print was evaporating before her eyes.

"He's going to have to find Maryville on his own. And for all I care he can get lost out there." She dropped her room key on the counter.

"No breakfast this mornin'? Ya can't leave on an empty stomach."

"I decided to treat myself to a hot breakfast today. Any suggestions?"

"Your best bet's the Pantry. Straight down this street for two blocks, turn left, and it's one block on your left."

"Two blocks then left one block. Got it. Lil, it's been nice knowing you. If I ever get out this way again, I'll look you up."

The old woman smiled warmly. "Ya do that now. It's just too bad things didn't work out for ya with your oil well and your man friend."

Ellie couldn't help but smile at that. "Thanks. You have a nice town here. It's been interesting. Good-bye."

" 'Bye, little lady. Ya drive careful on those roads, now. Lots of crazy people out there. See it on my TV every day."

"I'll be careful," Ellie assured her as she slipped out the door.

Lil had put her magazine aside and was poring over a counted cross-stitch when a car pulled to a stop next to the office. She watched as a young man climbed out and made his way around the car, opened the office door, and stepped inside. Lil hurriedly set her cross-stitch on the table next to her chair, stood, and moved to the counter, her best smile in place for the handsome fellow. ''Can I help ya?''

''I hope so.'' She could see he was agitated. ''Can you tell me if Ellie Regan is still here?''

The wrinkles on Lil's forehead multiplied suddenly as both eyebrows arched. ''Sorry. Ya just missed her.''

''Darn,'' he said under his breath. He checked his watch. ''How long ago did she leave?''

''Let me see now,'' Lil said as she examined the large electric clock hanging in the tiny waiting room. ''She left, oh, I guess about thirty minutes ago.''

He scowled. ''You wouldn't have any idea where she went?'' His voice was almost pleading. ''I mean, I think she was going to Rapid City, but I have no idea where. She didn't make a reservation or anything, did she?''

A slight smile betrayed the fact that Lil was enjoying her role a little too much. She felt like she did when she held all the right cards and annoyed her favorite card-playing buddy to death by studying them too long before she slammed them down on the table announcing ''Gin!'' as if she didn't know from the beginning she had a winning hand. She realized suddenly she might not have time for such games. The nice young woman might be finishing her breakfast this very moment. ''If I don't miss my guess, I'd say she's still at the Pantry havin' breakfast. But ya'd better hurry, ya hear, or you'll miss her. The Pantry serves up their breakfast fast.''

He was already at the door. ''Where's the Pantry?''

''Go left out here, drive two blocks, then left again one block, and it's on your left.''

''Thanks,'' he shouted as he raced out the door.

''Don't mention it,'' Lil called after him, a thin smile on her lips. She liked being at the center of such things. She snatched the receiver from the phone on the counter and punched in a familiar number, watching his car circle the lot toward the exit as she listened to the ring. ''Mandy, that you? Should be a pretty gal havin' breakfast there this mornin'.''

She made a face. ''Have ya got a crowd a pretty gals today

or what? Oh, she'd be maybe twenty-seven or eight, dark, short hair, cute as a button.

"She's there? Good. Don't let her leave.

"I mean it, Mandy. I don't care if she is all finished eatin'. Keep her there just five minutes longer. Somebody's gonna be comin' through your door in about three minutes lookin' for her. And, Mandy, call me back with all the details. Should be fun if ya know what I mean. 'Bye." She hung up, sat again in her chair, and picked up her cross-stitching, feeling very pleased with herself.

When Graham came through the front door of the Pantry, he was relieved to see Ellie standing at the cashier's station deep in conversation with someone at the cash register. He could tell she was agitated. "I can't believe this," she was saying. "I don't care if you can't get the register open. Just keep the extra change." She was sliding some bills across the glass counter. "It's only twenty cents anyway."

"I'm sorry, ma'am, but we have to keep a record of all our sales. It should be just fine in a couple of minutes. Sometimes it just needs a rest."

"Having a problem?"

Ellie spun around at the sound of Graham's deep voice. "What are you doing here?" She rolled her eyes. "Can you believe this? They won't take my money because the register drawer is stuck."

Mandy, behind the counter, breathed a sigh of relief that the predicted meeting had taken place. She pushed the correct button, and the register popped open. "See. I told you a little rest would do the trick." She took the bills on the counter and provided the necessary twenty cents' change. "Ma'am, I'm so sorry for the inconvenience."

"That's all right," Ellie said, and she turned to eye Graham. "I repeat, what are you doing here?"

"I heard this is a great place to eat."

"Likely story." She glanced back at the woman behind the counter. "I see Lil's handiwork all over this."

He ignored her accusation. "I've been thinking a lot about last night."

"So have I."

"I may have been a little out of sorts."

"I think that would be a fair assessment."

"I'm sorry. Well, I said I was sorry last night, but you didn't hear me because you slammed the car door in my face."

"Oh, did you?" Her interest was on the rise.

He was suddenly aware they were drawing an audience, standing, as they were, at the front of the restaurant by the checkout counter. "Do you suppose we could sit and talk about this? Maybe you could have a second cup of coffee, and I could have some breakfast. I hate to eat alone."

She checked her watch. "I was hoping to make it to Mount Rushmore before the afternoon crowds, but I guess I could spare a few minutes." The pair made their way to a table, and Mandy reached for the phone to make her report.

"I've been thinking about what you said last night," he said when they were settled and he had ordered the two-egg breakfast.

"And?"

"And maybe you were right. I should cut my grandfather some slack. It would be nice to know what happened between the time he owned an oil company all by himself and the time he sold out everything. And another thing. Most parents don't let their kids get taken off to an orphanage, do they?"

"Not without a fight usually," she agreed. "Of course, you need to be ready for the possibility that your mother was taken away from them for some reason you'd rather not know about." Her voice took on a slight edge when she added, "But I guess you already thought of that, didn't you?"

He laughed. "I have a bad habit of expecting the worst in things. That way it isn't such a surprise when it happens."

"You need to try just the opposite," she advised. "Expect only good things, and life can be a lot more fun."

He looked at her with such intensity in his dark eyes just

then that she felt a tingling sensation work its way up her spine. "I just may try that," he said evenly.

When the waitress arrived with his plate of eggs, sausage, hash browns, and toast, he dug in with such gusto it was as if he hadn't eaten in a month. He stopped long enough to gulp a long swallow of black coffee. "This is a good breakfast. So what'll we do first?"

She smiled at his sudden enthusiasm and the fact she had been included in the search. "We?" she asked.

He looked at her, his face pure innocence. "You said to expect only good things, and that's just what I was doing."

Her face reddened slightly. He was using her own words to his advantage. "Well." She hesitated. "I guess I've got plenty of time to see Mount Rushmore. I'd say we should go to the courthouse first. We can check on death records and maybe even birth records."

He looked relieved. "I already know Mom wasn't born here. Her birth certificate is registered in Cheyenne, Wyoming."

"Okay. Then we'll concentrate on death records. Depending on what we find there, we could try the old newspapers. You can't tell what we might find."

"Good enough. By the way, I have that appointment tomorrow with the widow of the sculptor who started the Crazy Horse monument. You can come along, and we'll see that and then Mount Rushmore. Sound all right?"

She hesitated again. "I guess so," she said finally, "but I don't want to be in the way of your work."

"You won't be," he said quickly. Suddenly he looked up from his breakfast, which was fast disappearing. "Hey, I don't mean to be taking over your vacation. You probably have more important things to do than chase around after somebody else's family."

"If you remember, that's the reason I came here in the first place."

"Yeah, but you were hoping for an oil well at the end of the chase. Right?"

"I was at first, kind of. But deep down, not really."

"Aren't you supposed to think only good things?" He had an eyebrow raised to let her know he was only kidding.

"Are you going to keep throwing my own words back at me?"

"Sorry." He was grinning now. "I couldn't resist."

"Anyway," she went on, "I did try to be positive when I came out here, even though I knew it was a long shot I'd ever find an oil well—a very, very long shot, I might add. But I pretty much gave up on all that after my visit to the courthouse." Her face brightened. "Anyway, this all sounds exciting. Like doing detective work or something." She grinned back at him. "Besides, as far as the oil is concerned, it isn't over till it's over."

He swallowed a forkful of egg quickly so he could add, "Not till the fat lady sings."

She laughed. "Not till the fat lady sings."

Lil looked up from her stitching as the Toyota pulled into the motel lot followed by the white car she remembered from a little earlier. She'd been expecting them after the call from Mandy. She walked to the counter and slipped a key on the varnished surface. Ellie pushed the door open and approached the counter with a sheepish smile on her face. Lil, looking a little too pleased, slid the key toward her. "I gave ya the same room. The girl just finished with it. Should be all ready. We'll worry about the credit card thing when ya leave."

"Thanks," Ellie said as she took the key. "And you don't need to look so smug. I know you had something to do with all this."

"Me?" Lil said with a note of protest in her voice. "I don't know what you're talkin' about. I figger a girl's got a right to change her mind about leavin' if she wants to. So I had your room made up quick just in case ya changed your mind."

"Uh-huh. And you wouldn't know a thing about trouble with the cash register at the Pantry."

"Is Mandy havin' trouble with that old thing again? I don't know how many times I told her to get rid of that piece a junk."

''I'm sure you have. Anyway, don't be making too much out of my staying a little longer. I'm just going to help Graham do a little research on his family.''

''A little research, is it?'' She nodded knowingly. ''He is a handsome one, though.''

Ellie was at the door, and she wagged a finger back at the woman behind the counter. ''Lil! Now you stop it.'' She slipped out the door and hurried to her car to unpack for what seemed like the umpteenth time.

Chapter Six

Less than thirty minutes later the pair stood at a polished oak counter in the downtown courthouse. They were waiting for a middle-aged woman who had disappeared into the recesses of the office on an expedition to add what she could to the LeClaire history. They could hear her sneezing as her search stirred up dust. "I've got it," she called back to them exultantly. She emerged from around the corner a minute later brushing dust from her dark blue dress and carrying two yellowed file cards. "Husband and wife," she said as she glanced more closely at the cards. "Jerome and Mary. That sound right?" She peered at Graham.

"That's it."

She slapped the two cards on the counter, kicking up small dust clouds. "Someday we'll have all this on computer, and it will be so much easier."

Graham studied the information on the cards, and Ellie moved closer in her effort to see. "I'm sorry." He slid the two cards on the counter so they both could read. "He died July 23, 1943, and she died the same year. On Christmas Eve." His voice suddenly was filled with emotion, which seemed to surprise him even more than it did Ellie.

"How sad," she remarked.

He picked up the two cards from the counter and held one in each hand as if, it seemed to Ellie, he were trying to capture all that had been lost to him by not knowing these grandparents whose only history was the date of their deaths listed on the cards. After a moment he placed the cards back on the counter and smiled at the woman waiting patiently. ''Thank you for all your help,'' he told her quietly.

''Don't mention it. I only wish it hadn't been such depressing news.''

The two retraced their steps to the car parked just down the block, neither of them speaking. Once inside the car, he broke the silence. ''That was strange. I wasn't ready for how much that affected me. I mean, I knew they were dead, of course, but not so close together. And on Christmas Eve.''

''I told you not to be so quick to judge. You said your mother went to the orphanage in 1942, you think. That would have been the year before they died. They both might have been too sick to take care of her.''

He nodded thoughtfully. ''That's certainly possible. I just wish I knew more.''

''That's what we're doing here. So what's next?''

When he looked at her, she could see the change that had come over him. His eyes showed a new resolve. ''I know this isn't going to help learn much about them really, but I'd like to see if I could find where they're buried.''

Ellie sucked in a deep breath. ''That's a tall order. You don't know what their religion was, so we won't know what cemetery they might be buried in. Then, from the way things sound, they may not have been able to afford it, so we probably won't find a headstone. In fact we'll be lucky to find any kind of marker at all.''

''I know all that, but I still want to try,'' he said in a tone that suggested that's exactly what he intended to do.

She nodded her agreement. ''Okay, let's get started. There's a telephone booth just down the street. We'll make a list of the churches we find in the phone book and start visiting.''

The search was a demanding one. They found ten churches in all listed. They were able to scratch three of them after a brief stop at each rectory only to find each had been founded recently or at least more recently than the forties. Four of the remaining seven had quite complete records listing membership, baptisms, weddings, *and* funerals. A quick check of those lists left little doubt Jerome LeClaire and his wife Mary would not have been buried in the cemeteries belonging to those churches. The other three required the most work of all. The pair had to find the cemetery associated with each of those churches, one of which was several miles out of town, and tramp among the gravestones checking names. Ellie felt least confident about these last because she still harbored doubts that Graham's grandparents would have a marker at all. Sad but true, she realized.

They completed the list after a fruitless search through a tiny cemetery not more than forty yards from the church affiliated with it. They climbed back in the car emotionally and physically drained. It was 4:30 and they had been on the go since mid-morning, stopping only long enough for a quick sandwich at a drive-in restaurant. More than once during the day Ellie had asked herself what she was doing on this search in the first place. Not lost on her was the irony that here she was searching for the grave of the very person she had believed, only days before, was responsible for a major upheaval in her beloved grandfather's life.

"Well, I guess that's it," Graham said as he leaned back against the seat, obviously disappointed. "Maybe they weren't religious or they were cremated or who knows what."

"I'm certain they weren't cremated. They didn't do that much back then," Ellie assured him. "And they had to be buried somewhere. I'm betting they're buried in unmarked graves in one of the cemeteries we visited."

"I guess it was a stupid idea, anyway," he said.

She looked upset at the thought. "Not at all. It sounds like you're finally trying to come to grips with your past. That's healthy."

He rolled his head on the headrest to make eye contact with her. "Miss Regan, please don't be offended, but why is it you always have to sound so professional? 'That's healthy,' " he mimicked.

"Sorry," she said, with a self-conscious laugh, "but, while you're talking about our professions, may I remind you that I saw you taking notes in that little notebook of yours while we were trekking through this last cemetery? And that wasn't the first time, either.''

He laughed. ''I guess I was.''

''I guess you were, too. So there!''

''It really didn't have anything to do with the cemetery. The notes I was making, I mean. I just reminded myself to mention in my article how friendly the people are around here. They have been, you know.''

''I know, but you had to make a note to remind yourself of *that?*''

''I don't take any chances.'' Graham sat up in the driver's seat. ''What's the matter?'' Ellie was biting her lower lip. She was deep in thought and hadn't heard what he'd just said. ''You okay?'' he asked loudly enough to regain her attention.

She glanced toward him. ''Oh, sure, I'm fine. Something just came to me. Would you mind driving out to the ghost town I told you about?''

''Okay, but why?'' He was interested.

''It's just a hunch.''

''Female intuition again?''

''Something like that,'' she said without giving him the satisfaction of letting on she knew he was poking fun. ''When I was out there the first time, I could have sworn I saw what could have been an abandoned cemetery. It never really registered with me at the time, until just now. Something out there reminded me.'' She pointed in the direction of the tiny cemetery they had just explored. ''The weird thing is, I'm not really conscious that I saw anything there. But there's some kind of an image. Maybe just rocks or something.'' She looked toward him. ''Do you mind? It could be a waste of time.''

''No problem. I want to get some pictures there, anyway.'' He checked his watch. ''And it won't be dark for hours.'' He started the car. ''So how do we get there?''

She directed him on the same dusty roads she'd taken before, only this time she saw the right turnoff and avoided having to backtrack. They pulled into the field used as a parking lot, but there were no other cars. They climbed out, Graham reaching for his camera case in the backseat. Already he was interested, studying the terrain for the best possible angles. He pulled out the camera and clicked off four or five shots of the path that wound through the town. He said he liked the way the light through the trees made a pattern on the trail. They began walking that trail climbing gradually toward the mine on he hill.

''Whatever I saw, I think it was on the right somewhere,'' she murmured as much to herself as to him. They walked slowly in silence, trying to take in everything around them. He snapped another half dozen pictures. The loud clack of the camera's shutter shattered the tranquility each time he aimed and clicked. Suddenly she shouted, ''There!''

He jerked his head in the direction she was pointing. ''What?''

''Right there. See?'' He followed her line of vision to a sea of grass perhaps fifty feet by fifty feet, its perimeter only faintly defined by what once had been a wooden fence. What had caught her eye was a flat stone, propped in the grass, and clearly identified as a grave headstone by the cross carved near its top. ''I saw one just like that back in town, and something clicked in my head,'' she said excitedly. They advanced toward the visible headstone and found they were certainly in an abandoned graveyard with other stones lying just beneath the level of the grass. Whether toppled by age or vandals, who could tell. When they drew closer to the one visible gravestone, they could see it had fallen on another stone which was supporting it.

''You were right,'' he said as he looked about him. ''This is one graveyard we missed. This isn't going to be easy.'' He kicked gingerly at the thick grass. ''I hate to bring it up, but this is pretty good rattlesnake territory.''

Ellie had been standing a yard or two away, and she made a leap toward him, landing almost on his boots. She looked up at him half terrified and half embarrassed. ''Why did you have to bring that up?''

"I didn't say I saw a snake. I just said this would be a good place for them to hide."

"I know what you said. Any sentence that has the word rattlesnake in it is enough for me."

He put an arm around her shoulder. "There's no reason to get excited. You wait right here, and I'll go get us some good-sized sticks. If we beat them in front of us, we'll let any snake warn us he's in the neighborhood."

She placed a hand on his shoulder. "If it's all the same to you, I think I'll follow along with you."

"Suit yourself." He made his way back toward the path they had left, stepping as much as possible in their earlier tracks. She was right behind him, with a hand lightly touching his arm as if he might bolt away. Once back on the main path, he, scouted about until he found two serviceable sticks, broke off any extra branches to make them perfect for their purpose, handed one to her, and kept the other for himself. "Are you ready? Why don't you start here by the path, and I'll go back over on the other side."

The look she gave him was a distressed one. "If it's all the same to you, why don't we stay close together?" She anticipated what he was about to say. "I know, there're more afraid of me than I am of them, but I'm still not buying it."

He saw the look in her eyes and knew it was useless to argue. "No problem. It'll take a little longer, but we have plenty of time." They set off near the remains of the fence, poking the sticks noisily ahead of them and then brushing the grass aside to read the inscriptions on the fallen stones. Most of the gravestones were slender obelisks seldom more than two or three feet tall. They were crudely carved and inscribed and had rested on tiny bases. That and their fragile shape probably accounted for their toppling, the pair agreed. Their progress was slow, and they said little as they made their way through the abandoned cemetery. It became obvious there were few buried here. It was difficult to read some of the inscriptions, and occasionally Graham had to strain to roll a stone to one side or the other to uncover the writing. "I'd give anything for a weed-whacker right now,'' he said. ''We could make short work of this.''

''I can't believe a cemetery hasn't been maintained better than this,'' she said ''You'd think loved ones would want to take care of it.''

''You're assuming there are still loved ones around who would care,'' he observed dryly.

They continued once across the tiny cemetery identifying what stones they could find in a swath maybe six feet wide. They turned when they reached the broken-down fence and worked their way back, knowing in their hearts that the odds of finding the graves they were looking for were exceedingly remote. Ellie stabbed her stick around the remains of a stone lying on its face buried several inches in the earth. Since there was no name visible, Graham knew he would have to turn the stone. He pried at it to try to free it. He was able to dig his fingers beneath it and struggled to roll it so another side showed. Ellie's heart skipped a beat as she read the name and date engraved from top to bottom on the side that was now showing—MARY 1943. ''Graham, look!''

He had already seen the name and began digging feverishly with his hands to find another lifting spot beneath the marker. He worked his fingers under the gray stone and tugged hard rolling it to its next side. The engraving, though clotted with mud, was still easy to read. They could clearly see the name LECLAIRE extending down the face of the stone. Neither said a word, but she scratched in the grass heedless, at least for a moment, of rattlesnakes as she searched for the pedestal that once held the marker. She found it just as Graham pulled the slender stone upright, and then he walked it to its proper place where it slid on its base and stood firmly. They both stepped to the other side where the name JEROME 1943 was plain to see.

''I can't believe it,'' he said in an almost reverential tone. He looked around him then at the setting—the trees, the grass, the collapsing houses—almost as if he were trying to etch the scene and the moment into his brain for later recall. Suddenly he remembered his camera. He dug it out of the case he had set in the grass and began stalking the marker standing alone in the tiny cemetery. He took at least a dozen pictures. That was Ellie's guess, anyway. She had moved out of the way, back to the hiking trail that led through the remains of the town. She wanted to give him his space, and he hadn't yet noticed she was gone. Finished with his pictures finally, he stepped toward the monument, stood quietly for a moment, and then suddenly placed a hand gently on the rough stone. This last gesture brought sudden tears to Ellie's eyes, and she dabbed at them with the sleeve of her shirt.

He looked about him, for the first time in several minutes seeing more than just the monument. He spotted her standing some distance away and smiled. ''There you are.'' He joined her on the trail, and the two looked back at the stone, the engraved LECLAIRE clearly visible from where they stood. He put a hand on her shoulder and pulled her close to his side. ''Thanks. You know I never would have found them if it hadn't been for you. No, more than that, I never would have *wanted* to find them if it hadn't been for you.'' She wasn't about to trust her voice just now. Her only answer was to slip an arm around his waist. He looked down at her. ''Did you know what this would mean to me?''

''I had an idea,'' she said softly.

''This is what you meant about coming to grips with my past?''

''It's a start. But we still have a lot to find out.''

That night over coffee after dinner—they were at the Mountain View again—the pair talked at great length about the day. Graham was still in shock at the unexpected deep feeling that had overcome him at the cemetery. ''I never even knew those two, but all of a sudden I felt so close to them. It's strange. And you.'' He grinned across the table at Ellie. ''What made you think they might be buried there?''

She stared across the table at him with wild eyes. ''I have strange powers,'' she recited in a monotone.

He laughed. ''Yeah, right, that women's intuition thing again?''

She answered him seriously this time. "It was kind of by process of elimination. We'd tried every cemetery in the town. I knew they had to be buried somewhere. Why not there?" A new thought struck her. "You know, I'm guessing that little community didn't last much longer than the mid-forties. I'll have to ask Lil. She'll know. That would explain why there aren't a lot of graves out there."

"That isn't such a long time ago. I still can't believe the place is in such bad shape."

"I told you. There are no families left to see that it's taken care of."

"Well, there's one now. I'm going to check around and find out what can be done. It wouldn't be impossible to put that place back in shape. The monuments we found weren't badly damaged." His face hardened. "If nothing can be done, I'm going to look into having their graves moved."

Ellie frowned. "I hope you don't have to do that."

"Why?"

"There's a reason they were buried there."

He took up that new thought. "I've been thinking about that. Why do you suppose they *were* buried there? I mean, they lived in town and all."

"I'm guessing they hadn't lived in town all that long. I'll bet they still had lots of friends in Maryville."

He tossed out an idea that had been floating in his head since the discovery this afternoon. "Maybe Grandpa was killed in the war. Did you ever think of that? Maybe that's why my mom doesn't remember anything about him. He could have been in the army for a couple of years. Just about everyone under a certain age was."

She nodded her head thoughtfully partly at what he'd just said and partly that she'd heard him call Jerome LeClaire "Grandpa" for the first time. "That's possible," she said finally, "but I don't think so. I still have a feeling there's something strange about his death."

"Sounds like that feeling of yours is starting to work overtime." He held up his hand when he saw she was about to object. "I know, I know, it hasn't let you down yet."

"Right. But there's an even better reason."

"What's that?"

"There's a monument in front of the courthouse honoring World War Two dead from this county, and Jerome LeClaire's name isn't on it."

"How in the world did you spot that?"

"I noticed it the first day in town. Remember, I was looking for anything that might have his name on it. You know, to find out if he even existed."

Graham shook his head. "You don't miss much." He finished his coffee. "So what's next?"

"You're not forgetting your interview with the Crazy Horse woman tomorrow, are you?"

He slapped his forehead. "My gosh, that's right. I would have forgotten completely if you hadn't said something. You're coming along, aren't you?"

She hadn't expected the invitation. "I don't want to be in the way. You've got a job to do."

"That's silly. I guarantee you wouldn't be in the way. Anyway, I promised we'd see Mount Rushmore. You had that on your list, didn't you?"

"Definitely."

"Good. Then it's settled. We'll do the tourist scene in the Black Hills tomorrow and then investigate the LeClaires around here the next day. Agreed?"

When she didn't answer right away, he was afraid he might be scaring her off which he certainly didn't want to do. Maybe things were moving too fast. "I guess I'm taking a lot for granted here. You must have plans of your own. I don't know why I should think you'd be interested in trying to research my ancient history." He grinned. "Especially now that you know there's no oil well at the end of it all."

She wondered where all this was taking her. She could guess what Erin would say. But the truth was, she was fascinated with what they'd found so far, and she definitely wanted to know the rest of the story. And, yes, it was true—she was beginning to entertain as much interest in the LeClaire family's present history as in its past, especially as regarded one handsome travel-agent member of that family. *So, we've known each other all of two days,* she thought. *They've been a couple of eventful days, haven't they? Even a pretty good argument thrown in.* In that instant of reflection she'd made up her mind but went for the light touch. "No, I'd like to go. Really. Anyway, don't think for a minute you're going to keep all that oil for yourself."

He was relieved, and he laughed as he pulled himself up out of the booth. "Darn, I was already counting the money." He stretched. "Now, I've got to get some sleep if I'm going to be ready for Mrs. Ziolkowski tomorrow." He rubbed his sore hands gingerly. "I don't know if I'll be able to hold a pen. I haven't done this much work in ten years."

Chapter Seven

Graham dropped by the Pine Rest for Ellie the next morning at precisely eight o'clock. He had an appointment with Mrs. Ziolkowski at 10:00, and they both had agreed the night before that two hours would allow plenty of time for the drive. Lil waved from her perch in the motel office as the car headed out. Ellie waved back. Lil had come on duty while she was eating her solitary breakfast in the tiny office dining room, and Ellie brought her up-to-date on the latest—namely, finding the grave sites of Graham's grandparents. She nodded at the news. "So it's graves you're huntin' for now," she observed. "You've given up on findin' oil, I see. And how are things progressin' with that man friend of yours?" she asked pointedly. "He's a handsome one, he is." Ellie had ignored Lil's question, expressing shock at the time and hurrying back to her room to brush her teeth, apply a wisp of makeup, and run a comb through her hair.

Now they were on their way back through town, following the same route Ellie had taken. *What was it,* she asked herself, *just three days ago?* So much had happened in such a short time, she thought. The drive was a delight. They chatted easily about many things. Graham told her about some of the places he'd visited, and she knew he could have gone on forever with such accounts. But he seemed just as interested in her stories, though for the life of her, she couldn't imagine why. She told him about her friends and the things they enjoyed

100

doing back in Dubuque, a city he admitted to never having visited unless she would let him count an interstate drive-by some eight years ago on the way to the Wisconsin Dells.

She expressed genuine surprise. "I can't believe you've never done a single travel story on little old Dubuque," she chided him. "And you call yourself a travel writer. There are lots of things to see there."

He looked toward her, a mischievous grin playing at his lips. "What, are you on the travel bureau or something?"

She shifted in her seat. "No, I mean it. It's a beautiful place."

"I'm sure it is. I've just never had the pleasure of going there, and it isn't really all that far from Chicago." An idea struck him just then. "If you'll be my travel guide, I'll see if I can do an article on it."

The idea excited her. "Do you mean it?"

"Of course I mean it."

"And you'll get it in a magazine and everything?"

He laughed. "Well, now, that's not automatic. But I'll try. You have to come up with some kind of angle that we can work on. You know, like something that's a big deal in Dubuque. National Pizza Day or a chili cook-off that people flock to from thousands of miles away. You know, something like that. Naturally, we'll be looking toward publication next year because most magazines are working anywhere from three to six months in advance."

"Really?"

"Definitely. Sometimes longer. So we'd plan to cover it this summer or fall or whenever it is and then get it in the magazine for readers to include in their travel plans for the next year."

"So that's how it works?" Her mind was already working on the assignment.

"That's how it works. So then the article centers on that activity, whatever it is, but includes a travel guide about all the other things to see while the reader is there."

"But you don't do that with everything. Like if you're doing a story on Paris."

He laughed. "You're right. You don't need much to tie in a story about Paris. But that's not always true. I've got an assignment to go to Rome next spring to research places to stay during the big millennium celebration. They're expecting something like thirty million people in the city that year, and they're opening up monasteries and convents and places like that to handle the crowds. So I'm doing a piece on finding alternative accommodations. You know—how to arrange for them in advance, how much they're going to cost. Stuff like that."

"That sounds like a great idea."

His face showed he was pleased. "I'm glad you like it. I think its pretty good, too. It could get good play. I hope it works out."

"Rome," she said with a sigh as she gazed out the window at the passing scenery. "That sounds so exciting. Have you been there before?"

He wrinkled his face in thought. "Three times."

"Three times?!"

"Yup."

"Is it beautiful?"

"Very much so." He looked over at her. "And unbelievably crowded, at least in the summer."

They rode on in silence for a few minutes, deep in their own thoughts. Ellie was searching her brain for the proper tie-in for an article about Dubuque. Graham was thinking about the article himself but for a different reason. He knew their research into his family history couldn't last forever. They would both go home eventually, and he wasn't pleased at the prospect of leaving this young woman. An article about her hometown would give him the perfect reason to visit. They would have to plan an outline for the article, check on possible sources, scope out some picture possibilities. Such planning could take the better part of the summer, he decided. Had Graham Stahmers, the confirmed bachelor, finally met his match? Wouldn't the bunch back home enjoy the sound of that, he thought. It was strange. They had met only two days ago and yet he felt he had known Ellie forever. Was it because of her interest in his long-lost family? And why was she so interested in finding out about a man who obviously had taken advantage of her grandfather? He took his eyes off the road and glanced in her direction, surprised to find her studying him. Their eyes met and they smiled at each other.

They drove on and caught the interstate shortly after crossing the South Dakota state line. Graham stopped once at a scenic pulloff to jot something in his ever-present notebook. He said it was just description that he might use in one of the articles on the Black Hills. They rolled past Deadwood. ''I want to stop there on my way home,'' Ellie said.

''Deadwood?''

''Yes, it looks interesting.''

''We could have stopped now if it weren't for my appointment.''

''That's okay.''

''It's an interesting town. You can see the bar where Wild Bill was killed and even the hand of cards he was holding. The whole place is one big casino now, though.''

''You've been here before?''

''Um-hm,'' he said. ''Several times.''

''And you've never tried to investigate your grandparents before?'' There was surprise in her voice.

''No,'' he said simply. ''Well, you have to understand I never knew they were from around here until not very long ago. It wasn't something Mom ever talked about.''

Ellie nodded. She was thinking how grateful she was to have known both sets of grandparents. She knew she wouldn't give that up for all the oil wells in Wyoming. She glanced up and saw the exit for Sturgis up ahead.

''Have you ever heard of the Sturgis Motorcycle Rally?'' he asked.

She shook her head. ''Can't say that I have.''

''It's wild. Held in August. You should see the motorcycles around here at that time. You see 'em everywhere. It's quite a show.''

''I imagine.''

''Now, that's what I mean by an angle for an article. Fifty-one weeks out of the year Sturgis is just a sleepy little town, but that all changes for one week in August.''

As they came within sight of Rapid City, a busy little city nestled snugly up against the famous Black Hills, from what Ellie could see, he took the offramp for Mount Rushmore, the one she'd noticed on her way through. They drove seemingly on the edge of the city for a few minutes, climbing at first and then beginning a long descent into a valley that she could see would soon rise again sharply into the Hills themselves. The roadside was dotted with billboards proclaiming caves and water slides and old-time railroads. ''There's something coming up on your right you might enjoy,'' Graham said as he pointed.

She saw a huge glass dome and a sign proclaiming Reptile Gardens. ''I think I'll give that a miss,'' she said. Now they began the long climb into the Black Hills themselves. ''Are we going to see Mount Rushmore first?'' She was checking her watch. ''There's not much time before your appointment.''

''We have to go right by it before we get to Crazy Horse, but we'll stop on the way back. Now, be ready to look off to your right when we get around this curve. Right about *now!*''

She bent her head to take in the whole scope of the mountains through the windshield as they swept around the bend, and there they were, the four faces, white against the blue sky which was their backdrop. Graham was watching for her reaction. ''What'd you think?''

''They're beautiful,'' she said with less enthusiasm than he had hoped.

''That's all?'' he said, obviously disappointed.

She was trying to keep the carvings in view as the car made another turn. ''They're not as big as I thought they were going to be.''

He spotted a scenic-view parking spot just ahead and pulled off. ''That's because we're so far away. Wait till we get closer. Then you'll see them the way you're used to seeing them in all the pictures.''

They sat for a moment as she took in the view. ''It is amazing. How did they manage to get the facial details like that?''

"Dynamite first and then hand drills to do the final shaping. Borglum's original plan was to show more of them so they would have extended further down the face of the mountain."

"Really? Why didn't he?"

"I think it was taking too long."

"You've obviously written about this before."

"A couple of years ago." He pulled back onto the road, and Ellie kept watching as the faces disappeared and then came back into view. They passed by the parking lot. "There's the new entrance," he said. "That's what I want to see. Do they look bigger now?"

"Yes," she murmured as she craned her neck to keep them in view. The road curved between granite outcroppings and Ellie switched her view to check the dropoff to their left. Suddenly Graham steered toward a tiny pulloff to his right and stopped behind a heavily loaded van.

"Now, look to your right and high up."

She followed his directions. "That is wild! I want a picture of that." She reached into the backseat. "Where's my brain? I should've taken some pictures earlier." She climbed out of the car and aimed her trusty camera at the profile of George Washington, all that was visible of the monument from this angle. Here was a view never shown in any of the usual pictures of the carvings. She climbed back into the car, beaming with excitement. "That was neat."

He smiled at her enthusiasm as he pulled back onto the road, realizing how much fun it was to show someone else such sights. The thought suddenly struck him just then that he did this very thing for a living, but he never got the satisfaction of watching a reader's reaction. "That's all for the faces for a while. Now it's on to Crazy Horse."

"How come the Crazy Horse monument isn't as well known as Mount Rushmore?" she asked as she slipped the camera strap around her neck, to be ready for another shot. "I've never even heard of it."

"That's because it isn't finished yet. In fact, it may not be finished for another twenty-five years."

"Twenty-five years?!"

"Maybe even longer. It's a family project. The sculptor started it all by himself, and when he died, he left it for his family to finish. In fact, he owned the mountain that it's carved on. He refused to take money from the government to complete it. I'm going to ask his widow about that today. I think it's still being paid for with private money." He gestured with his thumb back the way they'd just come. "Mount Rushmore was paid for with government money. At certain times there were a lot of people working on it."

She nodded her head. It was fun getting the background information without the research that usually went with it. She rode along happy she'd made the trip with him today. She watched the lush pines flash by, keeping a close eye on the hills about them expecting another of his surprises any minute.

They drove through a relatively low stretch of road, leaving the tallest of the hills behind and to their left. "Now, look back and to your right, and you should be able to spot Crazy Horse," he said. "He's looking out over this valley."

She twisted in her seat to check out the side window. "I don't see anything."

"It's not easy to see. We'll be turning in a few seconds." He clicked on his left turn signal and waited for an approaching car before he made the turn. He pulled to a small stand where he paid the entrance fee and then onto the long road leading to the hills in the distance. "There," he said as he pointed out the front window. "See it?"

She looked where he pointed, a reddish, rocky hill, and then she saw the strong face carved there. She'd been expecting a white figure standing out from its surroundings like the presidents' faces at Mount Rushmore. "Oh, now I see it. The sculpture is going to be the whole mountain."

"Right. Crazy Horse will be riding a horse and pointing off in the direction of this valley. See that shelf of rock that's just below his face? That will be his arm." He drove slowly, studying the sculpture. "I haven't seen it for three years. They've come a long way."

Graham pulled into the parking lot, and the two made their way toward a cluster of buildings housing a work area, a restaurant, a visitor center with gift shop, and a gallery of Native American art. They went into the visitor center and Graham asked for Mrs. Ziolkowski. He was directed toward an office area in the back. He examined his camera and the tiny tape recorder Ellie saw now for the first time. Satisfied, he checked his watch. "Looks like I made it on time. Will you be all right while I go off to work?"

"Of course, don't worry about me," she assured him. "There are tons of things to see here. Go do your thing."

"Don't miss the art gallery. It's a good one." He made a face. "I may be a while. Maybe an hour. Or possibly even longer."

"That's fine. I'll be all right. Really." She watched him walk away. He was wearing a pair of khaki slacks and a burgundy collarless shirt. When they got out of the car, she noticed he'd slipped on a tan sports jacket that had been hanging in the backseat. It struck her just then that he looked so completely in control. She smiled when she imagined the meeting he was about to have with Mrs. Ziolkowski, and knew that if she had a story to tell, which obviously she did, then there was little doubt he would get it out of her.

Ellie wandered through the gift shop, noticing several items she intended to buy for friends back home, but she didn't want to carry them around with her for two hours. She made a mental note of where they were in the store and then stepped outside and made her way toward a large maquette of what the finished sculpture would someday look like.

The maquette, placed in a courtyard not far from the visitor center, showed the famous Sioux warrior astride his horse and pointing into the distance as Graham had described for her. Behind this smaller statue across a valley maybe a mile and a half away, by her reckoning, was the mountain itself. Only now could she understand the sheer enormity of the project, turning an entire mountain into a memorial to the famous Native American leader. And, looking from the smaller statue to the mountain in the distance, she began to realize what had been accomplished. The powerful face was clearly there, the eyes that must have struck terror into many an enemy, so lifelike in their frozen stare across the valley toward the distant hills. And the other elements of the sculpture—the arm, the horse's head, the torso of the great Indian—clearly formed but waiting for the sculptor's touch to make them real.

She stood for several minutes studying first the smaller statue and then the enormous project in the background. Finally she shook her head in wonder and walked toward the art gallery. What a gift that must be, she thought, to make a whole mountain look so lifelike. She took a leisurely turn through the gallery enjoying the variety and quality of the collection of Native American art there. Finally she stepped back outside surprised to see how many more people had arrived. She purchased a soft drink at a stand and found a concrete bench not far from the maquette in the courtyard. There she could watch the people as they became aware of the scope of the project for the first time. She smiled at the shock of many of them as they looked from the smaller statue to the mountain just as she had.

"Been waiting long?"

She turned at the sound of Graham's voice. He sat beside her. "Not long. I've been to the gallery and now I'm just enjoying the people. And the mountain," she added quickly. "I didn't realize it was such a project."

"It *is* something, isn't it?"

"Where's my brain?" she said. "How was the interview?"

He smiled. "It went very well. No, better than that. It went fantastically well."

"Good. I want to hear all about it. Or do I have to wait for *The New Yorker* article?"

He laughed. "Let's not get the cart before the horse. Remember, that isn't a sure thing."

"I'm betting it is."

"Thanks. I hope you're right. Are you hungry?"

"Starved," Ellie said. "I've been smelling food from the restaurant for the last half hour."

"Could you possibly hold off a little while longer? Mrs. Ziolkowski has arranged for someone to take us down where they're working. I want to get a few pictures."

"Did you say *us?*" she asked with growing excitement.

"Yes, but you don't have to go if you don't want to. If you'd rather stay here and get something to eat, that's okay. I just thought you might—"

She cut him off. "Are you kidding? I'd love to go."

"You're sure?"

"Of course I'm sure. I've been sitting here wondering how they do all that." She pointed in the direction of the mountain.

"Well, let's go then." He led her back into the visitor center and out the back door. In less than five minutes they were squeezed into the front seat of a four-wheel-drive pickup truck with a jovial young man named Dirk behind the wheel. As he followed a well-worn service road toward the monument, he answered their questions.

"We use dynamite to make the big shaping. Did you see the picture back at the visitor center of what the mountain used to look like?" They both nodded. "Well, then you have some idea of how much of the mountain's been taken off to get us where we are now." He turned his cheerful face toward them. "Have you seen Rushmore?"

"We drove by it this morning on the way here," Ellie replied.

"They used drills to do the finer shaping there, and that's what was used here, too. But now we're using laser some. It's a lot faster, but the equipment's awful expensive." He pulled to a stop at the base of the mountain, and they all climbed out. Graham was already unloading his camera while Ellie stared up at the face above her in total awe. "It's huge," she said.

The young man, Dirk, couldn't keep the note of pride out of his voice. "Most people don't realize that from way back there." He nodded in the direction of the visitor center. "Did you know you could fit all four Rushmore heads in the space that Crazy Horse's head takes up?"

"Really?"

"Yup," he replied. "Well, look, it's gonna be the whole mountain when we get it done."

Ellie walked gingerly on the rock tailings that had been

blasted or drilled from the mountain. From time to time her eyes were drawn back to the face above her staring off into the distance, and she marveled all over again at the man who could conceive of such a project.

Forty-five minutes later Ellie and Graham were back at the visitor center relishing buffalo burgers in the restaurant. Ellie had insisted he try one. ''These *are* good,'' he said around a mouthful. ''Not quite as juicy as a regular burger but still very good.''

''Yum,'' Ellie agreed. ''So, do you think you took enough pictures?''

He ignored her sarcasm. ''I hope so. I still want to take a few shots around here before we leave.''

''You mean you still have film left? I've never seen anyone take so many pictures of one thing.''

''I never run out of film,'' he assured her with a grin.

''Remind me to buy some stock in a film company,'' she said as she slid her empty plate away. ''I'm anxious to get back to Mount Rushmore now that I've seen this. I want to compare.''

''The thing about Crazy Horse that blows my mind is that Ziolkowski worked on it the first years all by himself,'' Graham told her. ''He built a huge scaffolding on the mountain, and then he lugged all this heavy equipment up all by himself. Borglum had a good-sized crew working on his faces.'' He finished off the last of his soda. ''So, are you ready?''

''Whenever you are.''

''Okay, let's move out.'' He stood and dug in his case for the camera. ''I'll just take a few shots on the way out.'' They retraced their steps to the courtyard, meandered through the art gallery, and stood at the overlook for a time before heading for the car. Ellie kept track of the clicks of his camera this time, just for fun, and she counted twenty-eight by the time the two reached the car and he'd returned his camera to the case. *So that's his idea of a few shots,* she thought to herself as they climbed into the car.

* * *

It was just past 2:00 when they pulled into the parking lot at Mount Rushmore. The afternoon tourist crowd had descended, and it took some minutes to find a space in the multilevel parking lot. "This is all new," Graham told her as they left the car. "This and the entrance. That's what I want to see."

"And take pictures of," Ellie added for him.

"And take pictures of," he agreed.

They crossed the road toward a flight of stone steps leading to a row of impressive granite archways, like giant open door frames leading to the carved faces in the distance. It was an ideal photo op, Ellie knew, and she wasn't surprised when she saw his camera come out. "Just look," she said and nodded at the crush of tourists around them. Most were stopping, of course, to capture the framed faces for their family photo albums. Some were struggling to pose family members on the steps without getting parts of ten strangers in their viewfinders.

He grinned back at her. "I know. I guess that's why they built it. If you can't fight 'em, join 'em." He was brandishing his camera. "You stand right up there." He pointed at one of the steps above them.

"No, Graham, I don't want to be in the picture."

"Why not?" He raised the camera and aimed it at her. The shutter did its loud clack.

"What are you doing?" she asked with a grin.

"Just getting in the tourist mood. But I can't see the faces if you don't move up a couple of steps."

Reluctantly she climbed the required steps and turned back toward him. She discovered she was facing a torrent of people that parted as it came to them and then flowed around them. "How's this?" She had to practically shout it because of the clamor going on around her.

"Perfect," he called back. "Now, say cheese." He snapped the picture, and she suddenly remembered her own camera dangling from her neck. She brought it up to her eye and clicked a picture of her own, but this time of him. "What are you doing?" he shouted.

"Two can play that game," she said smugly. Laughing, the pair trudged on up the steps and through one of the doorways.

He stopped for more pictures, and she took some of her own. "This is beautiful," he announced to her. "You can't believe how different it is from what it used to be." There was a clean new building to their right, the visitor center, and beyond another row of granite arches though smaller than the ones they had just come through. The pavement beneath their feet was clean and bright and they followed it to a double row of pillars, each pillar with a different colorful state flag mounted from each of its four sides. They moved with the flow of people among these flags to a broad patio viewing area where it was time for more pictures because the carved faces, much closer now, were spectacular. Ellie could see a huge restaurant with lots of window space on their right, and on their left she was certain she spotted a gift shop. That would bear some investigation later, she decided.

Graham pointed to a boardwalk trail to their left leading to the mountain itself. "This is new. Let's try it." They walked the boardwalk side-by-side, a couple of tourists out for the day. Ellie couldn't help sneaking glances at him from time to time. His enthusiasm about everything around him was contagious. She didn't have to guess why he was successful as a travel writer. There was that little-boy quality in him that made him want to see everything. She was glad she'd come along today. It was far better to share new things with someone else, she decided. Whether she would help him continue his search for his family, she wasn't sure. It was a private matter, after all, and maybe he would want to go on alone. How she'd gotten involved in all that was almost too bizarre to be believed anyway. But at least they had had this day together, a day that had nothing to do with old graves or oil wells or long-lost grandparents. Or so she thought.

He turned to her with the excitement showing in his eyes. "Look at the view from here." They had come close to the mountain and were able to look up practically at the underside of the chins of the four presidents. Ellie marveled all over again at how someone had been able to capture such facial detail on such a huge scale.

Now it was her turn to bring his attention from such lofty

heights to what was right in front of them, not more than twenty feet away. "Aren't those the drill holes Dirk was telling us about?"

"Where?" He looked where she pointed. Great tailings of stone had obviously cascaded down the face of the mountain during the blasting and shaping with the giant drills more than sixty years ago. The holes or parts of holes in many of these chunks of rocks were easy to see. "You're right. That's exactly what it is." He turned to her. "It was never possible to get this close before."

It was mid-afternoon by now, and the crowds were at their height. But Ellie was determined to see everything while she was here. She was most interested in Gutzon Borglum's workshop where the displays finally helped her comprehend how the whole project had been accomplished from blasting to drilling to smoothing. In one of the glass cases she found a group picture of the workmen as they were about to ascend the face of the mountain for the day's work in their tiny gondolas suspended by ropes and pulleys from the top of the mountain. She called to Graham. "Look at this." He joined her. "Do you suppose they knew what they were really creating? That it would become something so big?"

"I expect so," he said. "It was a pretty big deal at the time. I mean, the President came out here to see it while they were working. Besides, look at their faces. They were a proud bunch, I'd say, from the looks of them. I think they knew what they were doing." She stayed behind to study the faces of the men after Graham moved on. She found the picture more than a little troubling. It was an old story with her. She got the same feeling looking at her family's photo album. People had been caught in a moment of time. She could see or thought she could see in their eyes their hopes and dreams for a lifetime. The trouble with the family album was she knew how many of the stories played out, knew sometimes the hopes and dreams had been destroyed. An uncle killed in a car accident when he was barely eighteen. A great-uncle killed during the last week of fighting in Europe during World

War Two and only two days from his twenty-third birthday. An aunt dead of cancer with four children still to raise.

She knew the same would be true of the faces in the picture before her. How had Graham described them? A proud bunch. And they were. They had reason to be proud. But there was more to their stories. She wondered how those stories played out. Was this a time in their lives they always looked back on with pride? The defining moment that everyone always talks about? Did they make trips back here with children and then with grandchildren to proudly point out what they had helped create? She supposed they did. And why not? She remembered what her grandfather told her to cheer her up. They might have been looking at the family photo album together; she wasn't sure. "You can't get through life without some bad things happening," he'd said, "but you've got to remember there's going to be more good things along the way." She'd always found that to be true. She turned suddenly to see where Graham had gone off to. He was far on the other side of the room, and she had to hurry to catch up.

They left the workshop and made their way up the path toward the viewing pavilion. They both stopped and looked back at the faces. "More pictures?" she asked with a smile.

"I think I've taken my quota. I'll tell you one thing, though. I could do with one of those ice cream cones." Two little boys nearby were working furiously on chocolate cones stacked two dippers high, too big for them, it was becoming obvious, and they were fighting a losing battle in the hot sun. The melting ice cream was out of control, dripping from all sides of their cones, onto their hands, and onto the concrete in front of them. "Can you do a better job than that?" he asked with a wink.

"I think so, especially if we eat them inside where it's air-conditioned." And that's exactly what they did. The dining area was spacious with a glass-domed roof through which they could see the fluffy clouds against the deep blue sky. But mostly they watched the people, and they both managed their cones expertly. "No runs, no drips, no errors," Ellie announced as she held the last of her cone before popping it in her mouth. "That comes from many years of experience and handling some nasty triple-dippers, I might add."

Graham laughed. "If I'd known it was a contest, we'd have gone outside for a real challenge. So, have you seen enough?"

"I think so. We've seen it all, haven't we?"

"We've seen everything but the light show, but if we stay for that, it will be late by the time we get back to Wyoming. I wish you could see it, though. It *is* something."

"I'll stop on my way back home. I probably should visit a cave, don't you think?"

He stood up and sank a shot with his rolled-up napkin at a nearby trash barrel. "Oh, by all means, and don't forget about Reptile Gardens."

She grinned. "I've got it right at the top of my list. Hey, nice shot."

They walked outside into the hot sun and back through the rows of flags. "Would you mind hanging onto my suitcase?" he asked, unshouldering his camera case. "I need to make a stop before we get on the road." She took the case from him and hoisted the strap to her shoulder as he walked off in the direction of the restrooms.

"I'll be in the gift shop," she called after him. He turned at the sound of her voice, and she wasn't sure he had heard because of the noise of the crowd. She pointed back in the direction of the gift shop and mouthed the words. He nodded his understanding, and she saw the hint of a smile, more of a smirk really, that suggested he thought it unlikely all along that they would leave the premises without a visit to the gift shop. Well, she would show him. Who needed the gift shop, anyway? She moved against the flow of people coming toward her through the granite entrance where they had taken pictures earlier. She would wait right here for him. As she stood watching the people, she spotted an impressive bronze plaque outside the visitor center. She drew closer to see what it was all about. The heading, in slightly larger lettering than the rest, read: *In Grateful Recognition to Those Workers Who Made This Memorial Possible*.

The list of names was arranged alphabetically, and she

scanned it more out of habit than even any real curiosity. She knew she must have expressed her shock out loud at what she saw because she was aware that several people stopped to stare at her. She stepped closer to the plaque and read again to be sure of what she thought she had seen. There it was in neatly printed raised lettering: JEROME P. LECLAIRE. She stood in stunned silence, and her thoughts turned to Graham. She couldn't remember in her life ever wanting to tell somebody something so badly. She searched the faces in the crowd waiting for him. Finally she spotted the familiar safari hat he'd put on after the morning interview to keep off the sun, and she rushed to meet him.

"Don't tell me you're done shopping already," he said, and then he noticed her face. "What is it? You look like you've seen a ghost."

She grabbed him by the hand and dragged him toward the plaque. "You're not going to believe this. You're absolutely not going to believe this."

"What? What is it?"

By this time she had shoved him in front of the plaque with the simple order: "Read!" She watched his face as he read and saw his eyes widen as he spotted the name of his grandfather.

He looked away from the plaque and found Ellie's face. "I don't believe it."

"Well, it's there in black and white," she assured him. "Or bronze on bronze or something like that. He was one of the men who carved those." There was a note of awe in her voice, and she looked back toward the faces which stood out so majestically over the viewing pavilion.

"I cannot believe it," he repeated, emphasizing each word.

She grinned at the look on his face. "You never know what you're going to find when you start digging around in your past. Sometimes it's bad, but sometimes it can be good."

"But I've been here before. How come I never noticed this?"

"It looks like a brand-new plaque."

"I know that, but still, I've done a couple of stories about the place. You'd think I would have run into my grandfather's name.''

''You weren't looking for it,'' she said simply.

''I suppose you're right. I wouldn't have seen it today if it hadn't been for you.'' He bent closer to the plaque. ''How did you see this?''

''I don't know really. I guess I spotted it as I was waiting, and I was curious.''

He took a deep breath, let it out slowly, and shook his head. ''Incredible. This is going to put my mom in orbit. I can hardly wait to tell her.''

The two stood looking at each other. ''So what now?'' Ellie asked finally.

Graham's face brightened suddenly with a thought. ''Pictures. I need some pictures.'' She was still holding his camera bag, and he reached for it.

She laughed. ''Of course. Why didn't I think of that?''

He had the camera in his hands already, and he took five or six shots from every angle imaginable when a new thought struck him. ''I've got to have one with you in it.''

''Me? Why me?'' she protested.

''You found it. Who better to be in it than you? Besides, I want Mom to see you.''

She was still thinking about that last comment when he took her by the arm and led her to the plaque. ''Now, put your left hand at the top of the plaque. Right. Good. Now smile.'' She heard the loud clack of the shutter.

''Hey, what about you? Let me take one of you if you think I can handle that fancy contraption you call a camera.''

''No problem,'' he said as he handed it over.

But before he could tell her what to look through and what to push, a smiling, middle-aged Japanese tourist, a long-lensed, expensive-looking camera of his own dangling from his neck, interrupted. ''I take?'' He pointed from one to the other of them.

''That would be very good of you,'' Graham said as he plucked the camera out of her hands and handed it carefully to the stranger. ''Look through here and adjust—''

The man, smiling broadly, interrupted. "I know camera. You and wife . . ."

He left his directions unsaid, but they both knew he wanted them to pose. But as she took her place on one side of the plaque, Ellie felt some duty to correct their helpful shutterbug. She pointed at Graham and then at herself. "No, you see we're not married. Just friends."

The man nodded his head several times. "Ah, friends," he said. Then he raised the camera, focused it with a practiced hand, and snapped the shutter. He handed the camera back with a quick bow.

Graham returned the bow. "Thank you so much." As the volunteer photographer moved off, Graham turned to Ellie and smiled. "That was nice of him, wasn't it?"

She nodded. "Now what? Do you still want to leave?"

"No," he said with a sheepish grin. "I'd like to go back to the workshop and look at that picture again. You know, the one of all the workers."

"Want to find out if anyone looks familiar, huh?"

"Something like that."

"Well, let's go then. Say, do you suppose if we told them your grandfather helped with this job, they'd give us a deluxe tour of some kind?"

"I strongly doubt it." They headed back across the pavilion, where Graham stopped for another long look at the faces. This time Ellie watched *his* face and noticed easily the change there now that the story of the carving involved him in such a personal way. They hurried on to the workshop and found the display with the workers' picture. They studied the picture for a full minute without speaking. Finally, Graham sighed and shook his head. "There's no way I'll ever find out which one he is or even if he was in the picture at all."

"That may be true. At least you'll probably never know for sure, but there's one guy in that picture I'd put my money on."

"Which one?"

"You don't see him?" At her words he studied the faces again carefully and then slowly shook his head. "He's got your smile and your hairline, and there's something about his jaw. I see *you* right away.''

''Which one?''

''You're giving up so easily?''

He gave her such an agonized look then that she knew she'd better not prolong the suspense. ''Okay, okay, second row, fourth from the right.''

He bent closer to the glass, studying the smiling face looking back at him. ''No! You think so? No, that doesn't look like me.''

''Spitting image. In fact, the more I look at him, the more it's you.''

He looked again, and Ellie could tell by his silence that he was trying to commune with a face from almost sixty years ago. She knew the feeling from her own experiences with the family album and wondered if he too was struggling with the ghosts of his past. ''He looks so happy,'' he said quietly, more to himself than to her, and then she knew for sure he was thinking of the bad times that were yet to come.

''Yes, he does. They all do. But why shouldn't they? Look at the adventure they were on. They had to know they were working on something that would last practically forever.''

''I suppose.'' He pulled himself away from the glass. ''I've got to have a picture.''

''Why doesn't that surprise me?'' she said with a smile. ''But can you take one through that glass? Maybe we could get someone to take it out of the case for your picture if you tell them why.''

''No, I don't want to bother anyone at such a busy time. I think I can get a decent shot if I use available light.'' He looked about him to gauge how much light he had and then moved his lens close to the glass. He made some adjustments, and she heard the clack of the shutter. He took three more shots, which she was becoming accustomed to, making an adjustment before each of the shots. He stepped away from the case. ''That should do it.''

She watched him. She could tell he was reluctant to leave. ''Anything else?''

He shook his head in continuing disbelief. "I tell you, I'm still in such a fog. I can't get over this." He stood staring at the floor. "I'd like to stay for the light show tonight, but that would put us back in Burnbridge pretty late." He said it more as a question.

Ellie shrugged. "That's okay by me. It didn't take us all that long to get here, did it? And anyway, I wanted to see the light show."

His face brightened. "Good."

She checked her watch. "But what are we going to do till then?"

"What do you say we take a drive through Custer State Park? If you want to see buffalo close, that's the place."

"Sounds fine."

He added to the plan. "Then we can find someplace to eat before we come back here."

"Okay by me."

"One small problem," he announced.

She shot a curious look his way. "What might that be?"

"I need to buy some film."

She laughed. "I wondered if your supply would ever give out. You can buy some at the gift shop, because I need to make a turn through there anyway. I'll have you know you shamed me out of going there earlier."

"Really? I had no idea I had such power. I was able to keep a woman out of a gift shop. Amazing."

She pushed him. "Oh, you!"

They climbed back up the path, crossed the pavilion, and went straight for the gift shop. There she bought a couple of things for folks back home while he picked out his film. As they were on the way out the door, they passed a rack of postcards, and she remembered she had promised to send cards to her gang of friends. They stopped so she could make her selections. "Maybe I can write these when we stop to eat," she told him as they left the store. "I've got stamps with me, and I can mail them here, I think."

He nodded. "I saw a mail drop by the restaurant." Their

path beneath the arch took them by the bronze plaque, and she was amused to see him stop to check it once again.

"Is his name still there?" she asked with a laugh.

He looked sideways at her and reached for her hand as they walked. "Yes, still there."

They were going down the steps when a silly thought struck her. "Do you send postcards from all the places you visit?"

"No, not usually. Why?"

"Oh, no reason. I was just thinking that someone who knows you would have a pretty good collection."

He glanced at her, wondering what she was really asking and trying to decide how best to answer her. "Oh, if I see something I think my mom will like, I buy it for her. She has a collection of cups and saucers—which reminds me, I haven't found anything for her yet."

They were in the parking garage, and Ellie, who had been listening carefully to what he was saying, saw the white Ford up ahead. "Well, you should have looked at that gift shop. I saw a nice display of cups and saucers there."

"Really?"

"Yes. They were in the back next to that case of Black Hills gold I was looking at."

He unlocked the car and held the door for her. "I'll have to take care of that little matter when we come back."

"You mean after you check the plaque again?" she said as she slipped into the seat and smiled up at him.

"Maybe. Have you got a problem with that?" He grinned down at her and then cut off any possible answer with a slam of the door.

Graham edged the car carefully onto the shoulder of the road. "Roll down the window and get a picture."

Ellie looked at him in surprise. "Are you kidding? I could reach out and touch him." They were parked ten feet from the biggest buffalo she had ever seen, ever in pictures.

Graham was enjoying it all. "He won't hurt you. He's more afraid of you than you are of him."

"Where have I heard that one before?"

"Besides, they can't see very well."

"Now, I always wonder when people say stuff like that. How do they really know what a buffalo sees? You can't give a buffalo an eye test."

"Oh, they must have ways. Hurry up. Get a picture before he moves away."

She looked out the window at the animal hunkered down in the short grass so close to the car with his back partly toward them. "He doesn't look like he's in any hurry to move anytime soon." She fumbled for the window button, pushed it, and the window moved down slowly with a soft whir. Suddenly the beast shook his shaggy head from side to side, apparently locating the sound, and stared, Ellie was positive, directly at her with what she was convinced was a wild look in his eyes.

She squealed and slid away from the open window. "He can too see!" she shouted. "He's looking right at me."

Graham was doubled over with laughter on his side of the car. "The sound attracted his attention, that's all. He probably sees just some big white shape. Go ahead, take his picture."

She had never been this close to a buffalo, and her curiosity finally overcame her nervousness. She slid back toward the open window and studied the shaggy head. "He is kind of cute. Poor thing, the flies are bothering him." There was a swarm of the persistent insects circling his head.

"Aren't you going to take his picture?"

She brought her camera up, did her best to get all of him squeezed into the viewfinder, and snapped the shutter. "Got him."

"Wait," Graham said, "don't roll up the window. Take one with my camera." He reached in the backseat for his case.

"I don't know how to use your camera."

"There's nothing to it," he said as he placed it in her hands. "Just look through there."

She raised the viewfinder to her eye. "He's all blurry."

"Just turn the barrel of the lens." He reached across to show her. "Until he comes into sharp focus."

"There he is. Come on, big guy, smile. Now he's perfect."

"Okay, good. Now push the release just by your right forefinger."

She took the camera away to find the release, as he called it. "This?"

"That's right." She put the viewfinder to her eye again. "Make sure he's still in focus."

"He is."

"Then push."

She punched the release, and the shutter made its loud clack. Whether spooked by the sound or just because it was time to move on, the shaggy fellow struggled to his feet just then. Ellie was still peering at him through the viewfinder, and he looked even bigger at such close range than he actually was. "He's coming this way!" she shouted as she ducked away from the camera and tried frantically to find the button for the window. She heard Graham laugh, and when she glanced back out the still-open window, the buffalo was standing quietly with his tail-end facing the car. There was a small herd of his friends grazing uphill from the road, and something in that direction seemed to have his attention for the moment.

Graham was still laughing. "I don't think he's coming our way unless he's going to back into us."

"Oh, stop it," she said, a little embarrassed now at her outburst.

He pointed out the window at their rear view of the animal. "Have you ever been mooned by a buffalo before?" he asked, unwilling to let her off the hook so easily.

"Okay, okay, you've made your point. I may have over-reacted a little bit."

"A little bit?"

"Well, it's this darn camera of yours." She handed it over to him. "Everything looks so big through that thing."

"Did you get a picture?"

"I think so." She screwed up her face as she met his eyes. "It might be just a little bit blurry, though. I think my hand slipped just as I took it."

"You mean your hand shook, don't you?"

"Well, maybe that, too." She feigned indignation. "So sue

me. Now you know not to send me into the jungle to cover one of your *National Geographic* articles.''

''I'll make a note of that.'' He pretended to be writing in an imaginary notebook. ''Add buffalo to the list that contains rattlesnakes.''

''Definitely rattlesnakes,'' she said with feeling.

''Anything else you might want me to include?'' he asked, the imaginary pencil held ready

''Spiders,'' she said without a moment's hesitation.

''Hairy ones?''

She laughed at that. ''Hairy or bald, makes no difference to me. I just don't like spiders—period.''

He wrote in the air. ''Any spiders.'' He grinned at her. ''I don't much care for them myself.'' He put his hand to his chin in a theatrical thoughtful pose. ''I remember one time on an assignment a big hairy tarantula got inside my sleeping bag. I had to grab him—''

''I don't want to hear about it.'' She clamped her hands over her ears. ''La, la, la, la,'' she sang to herself tonelessly to drown out the sound of his voice. When she glanced back at him, he wasn't talking but he was smiling, and she guessed it was safe to take her hands away.

''If you don't want to hear a good story, that's okay. It's your loss. Say good-bye to Billy Buffalo.'' He nodded out the window where the shaggy fellow was plodding off up the hill to join his friends.

''Good bye, Billy,'' she called out at him as she found the right button, and the window slowly whirred shut.

Graham pulled the car back onto the road, and they were off again. At the next turn her curiosity finally got the better of her. ''Did you really have a tarantula in your sleeping bag?''

He looked sideways at her and grinned a devilish grin. ''No, but I did see one once in a zoo.''

''You mean you made that whole thing up?''

''Uh-huh.''

''Mr. Stahmers, I'm afraid I won't be able to trust you again after that whopper.''

He smiled but kept his eyes on the road ahead. They were coming to one of Custer's famed one-way tunnels, and he had to slow to watch for cars that might be entering from the opposite direction. "Honk the horn!" Ellie pleaded as they crept into the entrance and he complied. They both laughed when a van just behind them, loaded with Mom and Dad and a swarm of kids, followed suit.

They burst back out into the sunlight, and Ellie insisted Graham pull off so she could take a picture of the tunnel which, it was easy to see, had been cut through a huge section of mountain that had been in the way of the road builders. She took a picture with her camera and four with his, after listening nervously to his suggestions about finding the most creative angles for her shots. Ellie had never been particularly creative with a camera, and she doubted that was going to change even with the advice of someone like Graham who obviously knew what he was doing behind the viewfinder. The thought that he might use some of these photos to accompany his articles didn't do a thing to make her feel more confident. "If I get paid for any of these, I'll be sure to send you a check," he said in all seriousness.

"Right. I'm sure that's likely to happen," she replied sarcastically. "All I'm doing is pushing the button—I mean, the shutter release," she corrected herself with a flick of an eyelid in his direction. "You're doing everything else."

"I didn't say a word about that last one you just took. I think you're catching on."

"I hate to have to burst your bubble, but I think I forgot to adjust that focus thingy. There's just too much stuff to remember. Give me my old point-and-shoot any day." He shook his head in amusement as she handed him the camera.

They stopped for more pictures in the middle of the Needles, with its strange spirelike rock formations that seemed to defy gravity. They stopped for a lemonade at a rustic snack and curio shop set just off the road in a grove of pines. Ellie took advantage of the opportunity, while they sat at a table, to jot off her postcards, and she even found a mail drop near the checkout counter and then worried when they left that her cards might not be picked up for delivery for days. Continuing on they made a stop at Sylvan Lake, and deciding they couldn't resist the beauty of the spot, they set off to hike the well-marked trail around the mirror-smooth lake. By the time they came within sight of the car, the two of them were dragging. "I don't know about you," Ellie said, "but I'm starved."

Graham checked his watch. "So am I, but it *is* past six-thirty. I can't believe it's that late. Let's push on into Custer and see what we can find." What they found in the little town of Custer was a pleasant restaurant, off the main road, that specialized in Italian cuisine. They came upon it quite by accident when Graham made a wrong turn just as they entered the town from the east. The food was excellent and the portions generous, much to their mutual satisfaction. By the time they got on the road again it was nearly 8:30, and they had a twenty-five mile drive back to Mount Rushmore. Graham was already eying the sun which was beginning to slide close to the western horizon. "I hope we make it back for the light show," he said.

"We've got plenty of time," she assured him. "It doesn't get totally dark for quite a while yet."

Suddenly he pointed out the front window. "There's Crazy Horse again."

Ellie was surprised as she studied the face in the distance. "I thought I saw some signs for it. So we've made one big circle since this morning."

"Right."

"That shows how observant I am." She had the luxury of being able to watch the face on her side of the car as they passed by some miles away. Graham could only catch quick glances at it as he concentrated on the road. "Look at how the sun is shining on his face right now." She noticed that Graham had his head close to the wheel in an effort to see what she was talking about. "On second thought, maybe you'd better just take my word for it." She was quiet for a moment, and then the angle of the road made it impossible to distinguish the features on the mountain. "Won't it be something when it's done?'' Graham nodded his assent. ''I want to see it when it's all finished,'' she said suddenly. ''No matter where I'm living, I'm going to make a trip here to see it.''

''I will, too,'' he said simply, and the two grew suddenly quiet on that note of agreement. Graham finally broke the silence. ''Korczak Ziolkowski worked on Mount Rushmore, too.''

Ellie had only half heard him. ''Who?''

''Ziolkowski, the sculptor behind Crazy Horse. He worked on Mount Rushmore.''

''Really?'' She was interested.

''That's what his wife told me this morning.'' A thought, which strangely enough had never entered his head until this very moment, suddenly made its way front and center. ''Wouldn't it be something if he knew my grandfather?'' He found the idea incredibly exciting.

''He probably did. There weren't that many on the list.''

''He might have even talked to my grandfather about his plans for his own monument.''

''Listen,'' Ellie said emphatically, ''if I planned to turn a whole mountain into one huge statue, you wouldn't be able to keep my mouth shut about it.''

Graham nodded in agreement. ''Of course, he might not have gotten that idea until Rushmore was all finished, or he might have been like a lot of creative people who refuse to talk about something before they do it.''

''Or your grandfather might have suggested the idea to him.''

He laughed, but he could see the fun in her suggestion. ''Here you go again, finding the positive in everything.''

''No, I'm serious. I'm guessing your grandfather was a creative sort. I'm guessing he got excited about things, even the possibility of finding oil, and he had a way about him of making others get excited, too. That's the only way I can explain my grandfather buying into his wild oil deal and to the tune of a thousand bucks remember. I mean, think about it, even today would you give someone a thousand dollars if he knocked on your door and said he had this hot project he was working on?''

''No way.''

''Of course not, unless this guy was such a salesman you couldn't turn him away. I mean I knew my grandfather pretty well, and he never seemed the gullible type. Your grandfather must have knocked him right off his feet. Maybe that's what he did with this Zooli—''

''Ziolkowski,'' he prompted.

''. . . Ziolkowski. I can just hear your grandfather saying at lunch one day, 'This is all right, I mean four faces on the side of a mountain, but what would it be like to turn a whole mountain into one big monument?' And this Ziolkowski looks at him, and he says, 'Jerry, that's crazy.' '' She waited for some reaction, but there was none. ''Get it?'' she asked finally. ''Crazy? As in Crazy Horse?''

Graham gave her a look. ''I get it. And I'm beginning to think I kept you out in the sun too long.''

She raised her chin defiantly, but she couldn't keep from smiling. ''Well, it's possible.''

''I suppose anything's possible.'' Ellie's hand was resting on the car's armrest between them, and he suddenly covered her hand with his own. ''I want to thank you for what you've done. I never would have stayed at this thing, I mean trying to find out about my grandparents, if it hadn't been for you. You were the one who insisted I come to grips with the past, and now I'm glad I did. I still don't know a lot about them. I don't know why they abandoned my mother, but at least when I get home I can tell her something that should make her proud.''

She hadn't expected the conversation to take such a serious turn, and she had to swallow a lump in her throat before she tried to talk. ''And we're not done yet,'' she said softly.

They made it back to Mount Rushmore in plenty of time for the light show. Graham was even able to manage another quick look at the plaque by the main entrance and even buy a cup and saucer for his mother's collection. Ellie lingered over the collection of Black Hills gold while she waited for him to make his purchase. Finally, they hurried on to the outdoor amphitheater. They were able to squeeze into a place near the back. Ellie had seen the amphitheater in the afternoon from the boardwalk on their short hike to the mountain itself. It was nestled among a stand of trees directly below the faces. There was a small stage and a screen for early evening ranger talks. Though it had grown quite dark by the time they settled in their places, it was still possible to see the faces of the four presidents near the top of the mountain in front of them.

Suddenly the lights about them began to dim and the crowd, up until now noisy with anticipation, quieted as if on someone's command. As the strains of ''America the Beautiful'' filled the air from powerful speakers all around them, red, white, and blue spotlights focused on the faces above. The colors alternated from face to face while the patriotic music continued for some minutes until the first few chords of ''The Star Spangled Banner'' signaled the close of the program. Ellie and Graham stood with the others and joined in singing the words to the National Anthem. She felt Graham, standing so close to her, touch her hand and then take it in his own. The colorful lights that had been trained on the mountain faded slowly, then disappeared entirely at the instant the music and the words died away. Ellie turned toward Graham at that moment before dark turned to light. She could see his face only dimly as the lights among the trees and on the walkways began to glow to life slowly at first so as not to spoil the moment for the crowd. Or was it the glow from a thousand stars on a velvet summer's sky that revealed his face so clearly as it drew close to hers? She wasn't certain. Their lips met and they were suddenly alone in the midst of the milling crowd, the gentle breath of wind in the trees their only sound. When she opened her eyes finally—though it had been mere seconds, it seemed so much longer—the lights all about them had turned night into day and strangers, eyes averted and with thin, almost indulgent smiles, filed past.

Chapter Eight

Ellie dropped the two halves of an English muffin into the toaster and slid the lever down until it locked. "So how did ya like the faces?" She turned at the question and saw Lil standing in the doorway of the tiny breakfast room. She had been on the phone when Ellie had come through the office a moment ago, and the two had nodded at each other.

"I liked them fine. But you'll never guess what we found out." She was dying to tell the news to someone.

Lil's brow knit in interest. "What?"

"We found out Graham's grandfather was one of the workers who helped do the carving."

"Did ya now?" She *was* interested. "And how did ya come upon that?"

"There's a plaque near the entrance that lists the names of all of them," Ellie explained, "and his name's there."

Lil nodded. "And how did your man like that news about his grandpa?"

Ellie made a face at Lil's "your man" remark, but she answered the question as best she could. "He was shocked, I know that. We both were. I mean, it was just an accident we saw it at all. He said he's been there before and never noticed it. Seeing it was just lucky, I guess." She paused. "He was happy to find out something good about his grandfather."

"I 'spect so," Lil said. "Well, it ain't no oil well, but it's somethin'." That was about as close to impressed as she was likely to admit to. The outer door opened just then, and she turned to see who was coming in. "There're some fresh long johns in that box there," she said, pointing at the counter.

"Thanks, Lil, but I'm trying to cut down. I'll be as big as a house by the time I get home."

Lil snorted and waved a disapproving hand. "Worried about a little fat, and you're nothin' but skin and bones now." She disappeared from the doorway to tend to the person at the counter. Ellie smiled and shook her head.

Back in her room Ellie checked her watch. It was 8:30, and Graham would be by at 9:00. She decided to call home to report in. She had already made up her mind she wouldn't call her mother. Long-distance phone calls always seemed to upset her so. Ellie half-suspected the reason was her perception that such calls were an unnecessary extravagance. She relied almost exclusively on the U.S. mail, sending off a long, newsy letter to her daughter in Dubuque once a week and expecting an equally newsy one in return. Ellie was convinced that e-mail had been invented for the woman. It's just that she didn't know that, and it was highly unlikely she would ever find out.

She dialed her own number back home hoping that Erin wouldn't be out already, inspired by some new wedding preparation quest. "Hello," came the familiar voice of her roommate.

"Hello," Ellie said in as deep a voice as she could muster, "I'm happy to inform you you've just won a lovely honeymoon for two to a deserted Pacific island."

"Ellie!" Erin practically shrieked. "Where are you? Why didn't you call?"

"I'm in Wyoming, of course. And I *am* calling."

"I know, but you said you were going to call the minute you got there. I've been worried to death about you."

"I'm sorry. But you can't believe how busy I've been."

"Oh, of course, too busy to call your roommate. So what did you find out?" she asked with the excitement in her voice Ellie was hoping for. "Are you an oil baroness by now?"

"Not really."

"So that bum did steal the money from your grandpa?"

"I don't think so. He did have an oil well, at least."

"Really? So there was a man by the name of . . . What was his name again?"

"LeClaire. Yes, there was, but here's the part you're not going to believe." She said the words slowly. "I met his grandson."

"What? His grandson? You must be kidding!"

"Nope. Isn't it incredible?"

Erin's brain had just skipped back to oil wells. "So this is great news. He's running the oil business, huh?"

"No, afraid not. He's from Chicago."

"Excuse me? From Chicago? What's he doing in Chicago if he's got oil wells in Wyoming?"

Ellie grinned at her roommate's misplaced enthusiasm about oil wells. "Would you listen to me, please? There is no oil. He was as clueless about Jerome LeClaire as I was."

"His own grandfather?"

"I know it sounds weird, but it's true. It's a long story." And so Ellie told her roommate everything that had happened from the moment she'd driven into the tiny Wyoming town. She told about the stops at the courthouse and museum, the meeting outside the restaurant, the hike around Devils Tower, finding the gravesites, and the day in the Black Hills.

"And this Graham fellow," Erin wanted to know when she'd heard everything, "what's he like?"

"Oh, he's very nice," Ellie said simply.

"How nice?" Erin persisted, and Ellie could almost see the arched eyebrow of her roommate.

"Don't get any ideas," Ellie said.

"How come I can't get any ideas? Sounds like you and this grandson are hitting it off pretty good."

The thought of last night's kiss drifted into her head as it had persistently during the past ten hours, but she did her best to ignore it as she tried to reassure her roommate. "I knew you'd try to make something out of nothing. I'm just trying to help him find out about his family. He knows next to nothing about them. Well, he knows a little more now than he did.''

''Doing a little counseling work on the side, are we?'' Erin asked, and there was a disapproving tone in her voice.

''No, I'm not doing any counseling work,'' Ellie said, and her voice hinted at her growing irritation at her friend's insinuations. But it was just like Erin, she knew—always analyzing any relationship beyond all imagination.

For Erin's part she was worried about her roommate, hundreds of miles away as she was. It sounded to her like Ellie might have fallen under the spell of some sweet-talker who was probably as big a phony as his grandfather. ''What do you care about his ancestors anyway? I can't believe you've gotten mixed up in all this.''

''Gotten mixed up in what?'' Now she *was* irritated. Why had she called in the first place? she asked herself. ''It's just a good mystery, and I'm helping him solve it.''

''Well, have it your way,'' Erin said, ''but it sounds funny to me. A little too much of a coincidence. You just be careful out there and don't get hurt.''

This was too much. ''What do you think I am, some teenager?''

''Of course not, but you have been known to follow your heart and not your head from time to time.''

''Which is darn hard when there's always someone around to throw cold water.'' Ellie regretted her cutting words the moment they were out of her mouth.

''Sorry if I've been such a dead weight on your social life.''

''I didn't mean that. But sometimes you can be a little too protective.''

''I'm just worried about you. So far away and all by yourself. Don't let this—this LeClaire fellow take advantage.''

''It's not LeClaire, it's Stahmers.''

''I thought you said it was the oilman's grandson.''

''It is, but it's on his mother's side.'' Her tone had cooled and she was already ashamed of her earlier outburst. She tried her best to reassure her roommate. ''I'll be careful, I promise. Even about the heart thing.''

It was hard for anyone to stay angry with Erin for long. She had always been the overprotective mother hen of the friends ever since college days. She kept an eye on everything from exercise to boyfriends for the group, and Ellie knew her interest was always motivated by the best of intentions. Though at times she *could* be something of a pain. Ellie promised to call again when she moved to Rapid City, and the two friends, back on firm friendship basis though they had never been far from that in the first place, said good-bye.

Ellie set the receiver gently in its cradle and leaned back in the chair by the bed thinking. That was the effect her roommate often had on her in such circumstances. She always made her think, and most of the time that was a good thing, but not always. She had to admit, looking at it from someone else's viewpoint, that throwing herself into the search for Graham's family was a bit odd. Why had she done it? She forced herself to analyze her actions like Erin would have done and probably *was* doing at this very moment hundreds of miles away.

Well, first of all, there was the oil thing. She certainly didn't expect to become rich. Deep down she hadn't really expected that from the start, but there was a curiosity she'd felt from the moment she'd uncovered that official-looking document in her father's desk. Why had her grandfather, who always seemed so circumspect in all things, especially those dealing with money, made such a rash investment? There it was, a big part of the answer she could give Erin and herself. She wanted to know what kind of a man could have prompted her grandfather to invest a thousand dollars of his hard-earned money.

But was that all? Not really. She knew Erin wasn't buying such a simple explanation, and she wasn't sure she was either. Graham himself had a lot to do with her decision to help find his family. She knew she was more than happy for any excuse to be around him. The hike at Devils Tower, searching for his grandparents' graves, yesterday at Mount Rushmore and Crazy Horse—she'd found all of it so incredibly exciting. He was uncovering his past, and she was along to see it happen. She knew she would never forget the look on his face when they found the LeClaire name on the toppled tombstone or the way his eyes lighted when he spotted his grandfather's name on the plaque at Mount Rushmore.

Was she meddling, as Erin suggested—interested in the mystery, the search, wanting to help? She was pretty sure it was more than all that. Was there chemistry here? What everyone was always talking about? She remembered the kiss. Maybe they'd just been caught up in the moment, but one thing's for sure, she couldn't remember ''The Star Spangled Banner'' ever having such an effect on her before. They'd said nothing about it on the ride back, of course, and she'd drifted off in the car after her long day of exploring. She awoke bleary-eyed back at Pine Rest, with Graham gently shaking her shoulder. She would never forget these last few days. If that was living by her heart and not her head, then so be it.

A light tapping on the door brought Ellie out of her chair. ''Coming,'' she called as she grabbed her purse off the bed and hurried across the room. She threw the bolt and yanked open the door. Graham was standing there with a broad smile on his face. ''Good morning,'' he said.

''Good morning. You're looking bright this morning. You must have had your breakfast.''

''I'll have you know I was up at the crack of dawn this morning. I had breakfast and even took a long walk.''

''Well, good for you. I thought you weren't a morning person?''

''I'm not. Don't know what got into me this morning.''

They were still standing in the doorway, and she stepped outside and pulled the door closed after her. She suddenly hesitated. ''Do you think I'll need my camera?'' she asked.

''I wouldn't think so. Who knows how long we'll be in the library. We can stop by here if we decide to do any sight-seeing.''

Satisfied, she followed him to the car, and they were off in search of the town's library. Ellie had taken along a small map of the town, and they used it as their guide. ''Thanks for all your help on this,'' he said as he glanced her way.

Erin's question about why she was so interested in helping

a man she had met scarcely three days ago was still on her mind when she said, as much to herself as to him, "I guess I want to see how all this plays out. As long as I've come this far, anyway. Just call me curious. Anyway, it's like trying to solve a mystery. I should do this with my own family, on both sides, but I just haven't gotten around to it. I guess I'm learning how to do it."

"I'll bet you have a lot more to go on than I do," he suggested.

"That's true, but I would like to see if I could trace us back to Ireland, and that gets tough."

"You need to visit Ireland for that. Now *there's* a beautiful country."

She looked at him and shook her head in good-humored frustration. "Is there any place you haven't been?"

"Sure, but I'm working on it."

They spotted the sign for the library at the same time, and Graham slipped the car into an empty space just in front of the weathered, two-story brick building. "What year?" the gray-haired, unsmiling woman behind the desk asked brusquely when Graham explained what they wanted. They picked the years 1938 to 1943, and the woman led them to a locked cabinet, worked with an old key at the stubborn lock, and finally jerked the door open to reveal the rows upon rows of boxed microfilm on their edge, all identified with a year. She picked out the requested years and with the boxes cradled in an arm, she escorted them to a tiny room, more a closet than a room, Ellie decided, where three viewers were resting on three worn oak desks, each on a separate wall. She gave them a detailed explanation of how to work the machines over Ellie's protest that she was quite familiar with their operation and finally left them alone, making an obvious point of not closing the door on the pair.

Graham rolled his eyes when she was gone. "They must have built this place around her," he said.

Ellie laughed out loud. She was already threading the 1943 tape into one of the machines, and he was eying one of the remaining two preparing to do the same with 1942. "Is that nice?" she asked through a giggle.

"Probably not, but you have to admit she was something of a grouch."

"Not like the dynamic duo at the courthouse, huh?" She sat at her desk and clicked on the machine.

He looked up from his threading chore. "What's that supposed to mean?"

There was the soft whirring sound as she cranked past the leader on the film and arrived at the first page, brightly lighted in front of her. "Oh, come on now, don't tell me you didn't notice those two making eyes at you?"

"No, I can't say I did."

She glanced over at him and shook her head. "Well, they were still talking about you when I got there, and that was from the day before."

"Well, I didn't notice." There was an aggravated tone in his voice that hadn't been there before, and she looked up at him to see why. He was scowling at the machine with a length of film leader in his hand. "Darn," he said. "I can't figure this thing out."

She slid around in her chair and grinned at him, remembering his superior air about working his complicated camera. "It's not any harder than loading a camera," she said with just a hint of sarcasm in her voice. She stood and stepped to his machine, made an adjustment or two, and the film threaded smoothly. She clicked on the light and wound the first page into place. "There. Can you handle it now?" She tried to appear serious when she met his eyes, but there was a slight turn to her lips that let him know she was having some fun at his expense.

"Not you *and* Miss Battleax."

She couldn't stop a sudden laugh at what he'd said, and she clamped a hand over her mouth and checked the door to see if anyone had heard. "I'm sorry. I couldn't resist." She went back to her machine, and the two of them were quiet for some minutes as they advanced pages and read.

"This is going to take forever," he said suddenly.

"Don't read everything. Just look at headlines."

"I know, but some of these stories are a riot. Listen to this one. 'Local resident Earl Buxton was taken to County Hospital last Wednesday night with minor injuries after a run-in with a bull elk in his backyard. Mr. Buxton, upset after repeated raids by marauding elk on two newly planted oak trees, had stationed himself in his own backyard armed with a baseball bat to "teach them pesky critters some manners," according to him. Mr. Buxton was treated and released. The elk, who carried off Mr. Buxton's bat, has not been heard from.' " He looked over at her for her reaction. "Isn't that wild?" She nodded. "I can't believe they printed that in the newspaper," he went on.

"Why not? I bet lots of people had trouble with wild animals in their yards. Probably still do. Mr. Buxton was probably a hero to them."

"I suppose you're right," he agreed.

"This *will* take forever if you keep reading every story like that."

"I know, but they're interesting."

They both went back to their work. Ellie had picked the microfilm from 1943 on purpose as the year most likely to have some mention of the LeClaires, it being the year of both of their deaths. She could have skipped directly to the July issues, the ones most likely to have reported the death of Graham's grandfather, but that wasn't her way of doing things. She had no intention of missing any information and took the issues in sequence from the beginning of the year. She had reached July now and was reading carefully. Suddenly she looked over at Graham. "Listen to this."

"I thought we weren't supposed to read everything."

"You'll definitely want to hear this one." She glanced at him to make sure she had his complete attention before she started. " 'Local resident Jerome P. LeClaire passed away in his sleep last night after a lengthy illness. According to friends, Mr. LeClaire never fully recovered from an auto accident he was involved in while traveling to the nearby Mount Rushmore monument where he was working. He had been confined to his bed for some time. The deceased was well known in the area. He had worked the oil fields for years and was involved in the first successful drilling at Buffalo Ridge, a find that was to prove important to the area. He moved to Burnbridge not long before his accident, having lived before that at Maryville where he worked the mine there. He is survived by his wife Mary, a daughter Lucille, and an infant son Bernard. He was laid to rest in the Maryville cemetery.' ''

The two sat quietly trying to absorb what was in the short obituary. Ellie didn't know which startling piece of information to comment on first. It was Graham who finally broke the silence. ''That answers a few questions, doesn't it?''

''It certainly does,'' she agreed. ''So he was injured coming back from Mount Rushmore. What a tragedy that was.''

''I've got an uncle!'' Graham blurted as if that startling news had just this moment sunk in. ''My mother's got a younger brother somewhere. That is incredible.''

For some reason Ellie was glad he was most interested in his long-lost uncle. ''Do you think you'll be able to find him?''

''I don't know. I'll sure try. He must have been given up for adoption like my mother, but the question is where?'' His eyes were fixed on nothing in particular across the tiny room, so deep in thought was he. ''So she wasn't dreaming about that baby. There really was one. She's going to be so shocked. And happy and sad and hopeful and relieved and who knows how many other emotions.'' The look of deep thought on his face turned slowly into a broad smile as he imagined the happy prospect of telling her.

''We should have come right here after we found out their death dates,'' Ellie said. ''It would have saved us a lot of tramping around in cemeteries.''

''You're right,'' he said, and the look on his face showed that was another fact that had just dawned on him. Ellie could have almost been amused at the delayed reactions of a man who was usually so perceptive about everything. But when she remembered what a shock all of this must have been for him, she was more than understanding. ''Let me read that for myself,'' he said suddenly as he stood. She vacated her place in front of the projecting machine so that he could use her chair. He settled himself, and she pointed out the obituary near the bottom of the reflected page then stood behind him and rested her hands gently on his shoulders as he read. ''So he wasn't such a slouch in the oil fields, was he?'' he said with obvious pride when he'd finished. He looked back at Ellie for her confirmation.

''I would say not. It says he was involved in the find at Buffalo Ridge, wherever that is, but it must have been pretty important from the way it sounds. I wonder what all that means. Are they saying he dug a well there himself, or just found the place for someone else to dig?''

Graham patted her hand which was still resting on his shoulder. ''Are visions of oil wells dancing in your head again?'' he asked as he looked back at her this time with a smile on his face.

She was offended by his insinuation, and she slipped her hand away. ''I hadn't even thought of such a thing,'' she said with real hurt in her voice.

Graham realized too late the insensitivity of his remark considering all she had done in this search for his family, and he hurried to make amends. ''I'm sorry. That didn't come out quite right. I'm just a little crazy after all this news.'' As if to confirm that fact, he sprang out of the chair, wrapped his arms around her before she knew what was happening, and kissed her with such fervor that she felt more than a little crazy herself.

She finally recovered enough to push him gently, and maybe just a little reluctantly, away. ''What if someone comes in?''

''You mean Miss Battleax?'' He was grinning back at her with a reckless kind of look in his eyes. ''Who cares? What's she going to do? Kick us out?''

Ellie couldn't help but smile herself at the thought and at the way he looked. ''Probably.''

''So? We're done here. What do we care?''

"We are not done here," she informed him. "We still have a lot of things to check on."

"Such as?"

"Such as your grandfather's car accident. Aren't you interested in that? And we still have to look up Mary's obituary. Maybe that will tell us what happened to your uncle. And we might find out about this Buffalo Ridge thing. If that find was as big as his obit suggests, surely they wrote at least one article about it. If we don't find out about it here, we can go back to the museum. And don't you suppose the town paper would write something about one of its own who was working on the famous sculpture that everyone must have been talking about while it was being carved? Don't you see? The more we find out, the more we discover we don't know."

He had been staring at her in amazement through this lecture. "You're good."

"Well, I'm just looking ahead, that's all. I would think a good writer would think of these things."

"Oh, now you're starting to get nasty." He put his arms around her waist and drew her as close as she was about to allow in the possible vicinity of Miss Battleax. "I just want to know one thing, and don't slug me for asking. Are you thinking just a little teeny-tiny bit about the possibility of some oil?" She reached for his earlobe before he knew what she was planning and gave it a playful but still painful twist. "Ow!" he howled.

She clapped a hand over his mouth. "Sssh, Miss Battleax will hear you. You said I wasn't supposed to slug you. You didn't say a word about not twisting your ear."

"No fair," he said, massaging the ear. "You didn't answer my question."

She gave him a sheepish grin. "Maybe this much." She held up her hand showing a quarter inch between thumb and forefinger. "But I didn't think about it until thirty seconds ago when I was giving my little speech. So help me." She held up her right hand in trial-witness style.

Apparently satisfied with her confession of the very tiniest of greedy notions, he nodded to the two machines, "Well, we might as well get back at it. But I still don't think we're going to come up with anything as big as what we just found. And by the way, how am I going to find my uncle when I don't have the slightest idea what his name is?''

''Good question. I'll think on it,'' she assured him as she returned to her microfilm machine.

They stayed with their chore for some time, reading quietly, the only sound the quiet whir as they advanced from page to page. The only additional excitement came when Ellie found Mary's obituary. This one was pitifully brief, but it did shed some light on the situation of the children. They were mentioned as having been ''given up to the care of friends in their parents' time of need.''

''What in the world does that mean?'' Graham asked as he looked up from the reflected page with a scowl on his face.

Ellie was way ahead of him, already deep in thought. ''I'll bet some friends were caring for the kids off and on from the time the baby was born. Mary probably had trouble having that baby because of the shock of her husband's accident.'' Her brain was working overtime as she went on with growing excitement. ''In fact, it might have been somebody in Maryville who took them in. They probably knew more people there than here in town. That would explain why your mother doesn't remember much about that time. Then after your grandmother died, those friends decided to adopt the baby, but they couldn't manage taking both the brother and sister so your mother was sent to an orphanage.''

''How did you get all that from one dinky obituary?''

''Just reading between the lines.''

''That's a mighty big job of reading between the lines.''

Ellie was irritated at his lack of imagination in the matter. ''Have you got a better idea?''

''Well, no.''

''Then don't knock it. My little scenario fits what we *do* know.''

He nodded. ''I suppose you're right, but the bad thing is, if what you say is true, I'll never be able to find Bernard.

Whoever adopted him certainly would have given him their name, and we haven't a clue who that was.''

She had to agree he was probably right. ''We just have to keep looking,'' she said hopefully, though she had to admit the odds of finding Bernard's new last name were definitely against them. ''You can't tell what we might turn up.''

They went back to their reading until past noon when Graham let out a low groan. ''I have to stop this for a while. My eyes are ready to fall out of my head.''

''Mine, too,'' she agreed, and switched off the bright light of her machine. When they stopped by the front desk on their way out they soon learned the disposition of Miss Battleax had not improved much since earlier. It took all of Graham's sweet talking to avoid her demand that they return all of the boxes of microfilm to her safekeeping while they went to lunch including the ones that were stuck in the machines.

''She had a point,'' Ellie said as the pair walked down the front steps. ''We don't own those machines. Suppose someone else comes in to use them while we're gone? We've already got two of them taken.''

''I suppose you're right, but what are the odds there's going to be a big rush to view microfilm over the next hour?''

''You never can tell.''

He gave her a look. ''You're just trying to stick up for that woman.''

She laughed. ''Maybe I am. I just think it's funny you can't get her to fall for that cute smile of yours.''

Now it was his turn to laugh. ''I never knew I was so irresistible to women.''

''I find that hard to believe,'' she said without really thinking how she was leaving herself wide open.

Graham wasted no time taking the opening. ''So, am I having that kind of an effect on you?''

Her face reddened instantly, and she knew he had to notice. ''Let's just say I've watched the effect on others.''

''But you're immune?''

''I didn't say that exactly.''

''Could you spell that out a little more clearly?'' He was

enjoying this little inquisition since it was rare to catch her off guard, but more than that he was listening closely for her answer.

"I plead the Fifth," she said quickly.

He thought he knew exactly what she was saying, but rather than the satisfaction he had expected to feel at such a declaration of her feelings, no matter how guarded, he was surprised at the start of a nagging worry.

They walked around the block in search of a restaurant and settled on a little spot where they could get a quick sandwich. As if by mutual agreement, they steered the conversation away from themselves after they found a booth by the front window. "I've been thinking about what you said," Graham began, "you know, about the more we learn the more we find we don't know. Don't you think we've got about as much as we're ever going to get? Not that I'm disappointed, you understand," he was quick to add. "I mean, when I came here I never would have dreamed I'd be able to find out as much as I have."

She shook her head. "I can't buy that. We still don't really know your grandparents. You know what I mean—in any kind of personal way. Sure, we've got a lot of facts, but we need more detail." She arched her eyebrows and let out a long sigh of frustration. "We're so close, but think about what we don't know." She began to tick off unanswered questions on her fingers. "Why did he get into financial trouble? It said in the paper so plainly that he was in on a big exploration. What happened then? Why did they move away from Maryville? Why was he working on Mount Rushmore? Who is this Whitiker fellow, anyway?"

Graham shook his head, amused at her determination in the face of such an impossible task. "No argument here about what we don't know. I'm just saying we aren't likely to find the answers to the questions you're asking. I mean, if we were going to find out all that, we'd have to talk to someone who knew them. And we both know that's impossible. It's been darn near sixty years. Anybody who knew my grandparents would have to be better than ninety years old, maybe closer to a hundred.''

Ellie's face suddenly brightened with an idea. ''That's it!''

''What?''

''You're absolutely right. We need to talk to someone who knew your grandparents.''

''Did you hear what I said? If we actually could find someone who knew them, he'd be ancient.''

She was ignoring him. She had a hand to each temple, trying to make her brain work. ''His name is on the tip of my tongue.''

''Whose name?''

She was still ignoring him. ''William something. William, William, William.'' She was repeating the name trying to trip her memory. Graham shook his head as he watched her. ''No, it's Williams. That's his last name. Something Williams. Something Williams.'' She raised her head, and her grin told that she had it at last. ''Elmer Williams. That's it—Elmer Williams.''

''What?''

''I said Elmer Williams. I'm almost certain that's his name.''

''And just who is this Elmer Williams?'' Graham wanted to know.

''Lil—you know Lil from back at the motel?'' He nodded. ''She told me a couple of days ago that this follow Elmer Williams at the old folks' home here in town might have known your grandfather. Well, we didn't know it was your grandfather at the time, of course.''

''Uh-huh. And this Elmer fellow, he's about a hundred and seven, I suppose?''

She knew he was poking fun, but she pushed on with her explanation just the same. ''She didn't say. But she did say he had a good memory for things that happened a long time ago.'' Her voice dropped as she added, ''But he's not much for recent history.''

''You mean little things like what his last name is and what century it is. Little things like that?''

She'd suddenly had enough of his cute remarks and her anger flared. ''Well, have you got a better idea?''

He was surprised at her show of temper, finally beginning to understand just how serious she was about this new idea of hers, so he said with no trace of his earlier humor, ''No, I guess not, but I repeat, I'm more than happy with what we've already found out.''

''I know you are and that's great, but wouldn't it be fantastic if we found someone who knew them, to kind of fill in the blank spaces?''

''Yes, I guess so,'' he admitted grudgingly.

''Then we'll visit Elmer Williams?''

''It'll be a waste of time, but if you insist.''

Her face brightened. ''Good. We'll finish up at the library and then on to the home. What was the name of the place?'' She went back to the head clinching to try to extract this last bit of information. ''Buffalo Creek. No, but it's something Creek. Some kind of animal Creek. Creek. Creek. Creek.'' She released the grip on her head and smiled again. ''Elk Creek. That's it. Elk Creek.''

Graham smiled back, realizing finally how pointless it was to get in her way when she had her mind set on something.

After lunch they walked back to the library, smiled pleasantly at the woman still commanding the front desk without getting much reaction in return, and took up their posts again in the microfilm reading room. It took two hours to go through the rest of the issues they had set out, and there were few new surprises. Graham found an article on Buffalo Ridge, and though it was a lengthy one, it didn't mention his grandfather. He was disappointed. Ellie tried to find something positive in the story to cheer him up. She pointed out how important the oil discovery obviously must have been from the sound of the article, and he had to agree. But just what role Jerome LeClaire had played in the discovery, who could tell.

The only other important article—this one Ellie found—was about four men from the area who had gotten jobs helping with the work on Mount Rushmore. This one *did* mention

Jerome LeClaire by name, and Ellie was so excited she jumped out of her chair and started pacing around the tiny room. This article was a long one, too, and Graham slid his chair next to hers, and they each read quietly, that is until Ellie spotted the name Blaine Whitiker, and she couldn't contain herself any longer. "Do you see that? Whitiker? They owned the oil company together, and he's the one who bought out your grandpa. Can you believe it? The two of them worked on Mount Rushmore."

Graham nodded at all of these pronouncements, but his "I know" was mumbled in a distracted monotone. He was engrossed in the story, reading ahead, and, Ellie could tell, becoming more agitated by the second. When he finished, he turned to her and shook his head in disgust. "The guy who wrote this sure did one lousy job. He was so impressed with the whole business of blasting and carving the mountain he lost the whole local angle of his story. How many times was my grandpa's name mentioned?"

"Once," Ellie said. She was trying to hide a smile. She knew he had a point, but it was amusing to see how concerned he had become of this long-lost grandfather of his.

"I rest my case."

"This is a small town," she tried to reason. "Everybody probably already knew about these four guys. I mean that they were working on the Mount Rushmore thing, but they might not have understood the process of turning a mountain into a big carving."

Graham wasn't convinced.

"I still think he blew the angle."

"I will admit it doesn't tell us what *we* wanted to know," she said.

"It sure doesn't. We don't know any more than we knew before." On that note they went back to their reading but without finding another reference to the elusive Jerome Le-Claire. Ellie finished her last roll of microfilm first, rewound it, and put the boxes in order while she was waiting for him to finish. They put the room in perfect shape and returned the boxes to the front desk. Ellie nearly laughed out loud at Graham's final attempt to coax a smile from Miss Battleax with an excess of charm. His efforts fell flat, and she glared at the pair suspiciously as if they might be absconding with library property hidden under their clothes. Ellie barely made it out the front door before she was overcome with a fit of laughter.

He watched her, amused, as they started down the steps. "So much for my charm with women," he proclaimed.

"You overdid it," Ellie explained.

"What that's supposed to mean?"

"Oh, come on. You were pouring it over her with a bucket. She could tell you were faking."

"You think so?"

"I know so. She thought you were up to something."

"Whatever you say," he said, shaking his head. "So what now?" he asked as they reached the car.

"Elmer Williams, of course."

"And we will find him at—what did you say? Elk Creek Retirement Home? Was that it?"

"That's right. Now all we need are directions." A sheriff's car drove past just then and took a parking space three stalls down, and she hurried off to intercept the young officer as he was getting out of his car. Graham grinned after her, amazed at her determination. She was back in a few seconds, smiling broadly as she climbed into the car.

"You found out?" he asked, already knowing the answer from the look on her face.

She tapped her head with a forefinger. "It's up here if I can find the street signs." She directed him, ordering him to drive slowly so she could watch for street names. They had cut across to main street, taken it for several blocks, and turned on Aspen following the young deputy sheriff's instructions. Now they were heading away from the downtown section. Ellie was looking around her, her face a picture of concentration, when she suddenly shouted, "Stop the car!" They were passing a park just then, and Graham slammed on his brakes, swerved off the street to his right into a parking lot of crushed limestone. She realized too late her shout had been delivered with much more volume than necessary.

"What in the world is the matter?" He had thrown the car into park and turned toward her, not knowing what to expect.

She gave him a sheepish grin. "Sorry about that. I didn't mean to startle you." She pointed out the window. "But this is the place."

He patted his chest as if he were trying to jump start his heart. "You could give a guy a heart attack doing that."

"I said I was sorry."

His brow furrowed as he remembered her words. "What place are you talking about, anyway?"

I guess I got his attention, she thought with a smile before she started her explanation. "When I went to the courthouse the first time, one of the women showed me the location of your grandfather's house when they lived here in town. When I saw Aspen Street, I realized this must be it. Sorry. I guess that wasn't worth giving you a heart attack."

He looked out the front window at the park with renewed interest. "Are you sure?"

"You mean am I sure it wasn't worth giving you a heart attack?"

He gave her a look but also an appreciative smile at her little joke. "You know what I mean."

"Yes, I'm sure. She showed it to me on a city map. I remember it wasn't far from downtown, and it was on Aspen, like I said." He turned off the car and stepped out. She got out herself and watched him. For some reason her own thoughts on the gravel road in front of her grandparents' farm came to her just then. *What was that,* she thought, *two days ago? It seems like a lifetime.* Graham had nothing here to remind him of his grandma and grandpa, she knew. She couldn't decide if that was better or worse than seeing the slowly crumbling house where she'd had so much fun as a little girl. She was pretty sure it was better. Suddenly, she remembered something else the girl at the courthouse had told her. "Oh, I almost forgot," she blurted. "She said your grandpa's house sat about where that shelterhouse is." The shelterhouse, not much more than a roof of cedar shingles supported at its two ends by a crisscross structure of wooden timbers, was maybe fifty feet from where they were standing. Beneath the sheltering roof were six picnic tables resting on a concrete slab that had grass growing from cracks in its surface.

He stared at the shelterhouse and then looked at her. "Really?"

"That's what she said."

He walked toward the structure without saying another word, and she tagged along. He looked inside, stared up at the rough boards overhead, then at the picnic tables. They were made from metal and wood, the kind that have the seat planking mounted on curved tubular steel to make it easy for someone to slip between the tabletop and the seat. But she knew he wasn't interested in picnic table design. He was thinking about a house that had been at this very spot almost sixty years ago. *Maybe it is better to have something tangible to remind me of the past,* she decided in a flash, thinking again of the crumbling buildings back in Iowa. She was torn, though, the sick feeling that had overcome her at seeing the desolation of the farm nagging at her stomach again. *But he has no memories—nothing,* she thought.

He looked toward her just then and their eyes met. He seemed to read her thoughts. "I guess this is kind of stupid. There's really nothing here." He turned and looked toward the street as a new idea struck him. He wondered how much the property around the park had changed over the years. Not much, he guessed, from the looks of the old, boxy frame homes lining the street. And there were trees. Big ones that had certainly been there for years. Sixty years? He thought so. This is what they saw from their porch, if they had a porch, that is, he decided. He looked at Ellie again. "It's so weird. I know it's not much, but to think they lived right here." He looked again at the slab and the picnic tables. "I suppose the houses were all alike. They might have had a blue one like that." He pointed toward a faded blue house directly across the street from where they were standing.

"I'm guessing they didn't go in for those pastel colors back then," she volunteered, eager to help with his fantasy. "I'd say it was more like that white one over there.'' She was pointing to a similar house two doors from his blue one. ''See, it has a nice little porch where they could sit out at night.''

''Like they'd ever have time to sit out in the evening. He was digging wells and mining coal, and carving George Washington's face. And who knows what she was doing.'' He'd said it as a simple statement, but there was an edge to his voice that hinted at a bitterness about the kind of life he was beginning to realize they had probably lived. A life that was filled with more than its share of heartache. The kind of life that would end in early death for the both of them after the unthinkable—giving up two children for adoption.

Ellie put a hand on his shoulder. ''I bet they had a lot of good times, too. Your grandfather did some exciting things during his life. The obituary said he was well known. I'll bet he had lots of friends.''

He smiled. ''Maybe. I hope so anyway. It's just hard to think about the good times when you know how it all turns out.'' He took a deep breath and let it out slowly. It was a signal of some sort of closure. ''Shall we head on to our little meeting with Elmer what's-his-name?''

''Williams,'' she prompted.

''Sorry. Williams.'' He smiled. ''Mr. Williams isn't getting any younger, remember.'' He turned and headed back toward the car, and she fell in step beside him. Their hands touched, by accident or on purpose she couldn't be certain, but he folded her hand neatly in his as they walked.

Chapter Nine

The one-story brick retirement home was nestled just below the crest of a hill on the western outskirts of the town. Ellie wondered if there was an Elk Creek somewhere near to account for the name. Her best guess was there might be down in the valley spreading out before them. She could see the signs of houses probably built on substantial acreages, and why not near a river? she reasoned. They drove between the two brick pillars marking the entrance to the parking lot, and Graham slipped the car into a space marked for visitors.

They got out and walked the gently rising concrete path toward the front entrance where an American flag raised on a high pole snapped noisily with each rise and fall of the gusty westerly breeze. Five residents in wheelchairs sat on a concrete patio not far from the front door. Out of curiosity Ellie stopped and turned to see what their view might be. From such a vantage point it was impressive, at least in terms of the distance her eyes could take in. She could see the belt of trees below and beyond that the table top of prairie extending almost unbroken as far as her eyes would let her. There was a haze today, but she was certain that on clear days, especially in the morning, the snow-capped Bighorns would show themselves. Before she turned away, she noticed the black dots of oil pumpers like giant birds scattered across the prairie, some close enough so she could see they were working, moving their big heads slowly down and up.

Not the worst of views to finish your days with, she thought morbidly as she turned to see Graham was waiting for her. He held one hand to shield his eyes as he scanned the same scene that had caught her attention. As they walked closer to the front door, she stole a quick glance at the five residents and was disappointed to see that four of the five were sleeping in their chairs, their chins resting on their chests. *If Elmer Williams is one of those,* she thought, *this whole trip won't be too profitable.*

Graham explained the reason for their visit to a friendly, young receptionist at a desk just inside the front door. Her eyes widened with unexpected excitement as she listened to what the pair hoped to learn from the elderly gentleman. "Oh, I do hope he can help," she said. "He's one of our oldest residents, you know, and he doesn't get many visitors anymore." Her face clouded slightly. "His memory isn't what it used to be, but then whose is?" She laughed lightly. "He's better about things that happened long ago. I guess that's good for you. He has no family left, you see. He's such a sweet man. So courteous to all the staff. He'll be glad to have some company. I just saw him come through here not more than thirty minutes ago. And he's having one of his better days." She pursed her lips in thought. "I'm pretty sure I saw him go to the solarium, but let me check." She picked up the phone, punched a number, and waited, smiling at the pair in front of her. "Dotty? I have two visitors here for Mr. Williams. Is he still in the solarium? Good. I'll send them right in. Thanks." She hung up the phone and smiled up at Graham. "Yes, he's there. Go to your left down that hall." She pointed the direction for them. "The solarium will be your second door on the left. Miss Richardson is waiting for you."

Graham thanked the woman for her help, and the two followed her directions down the hall to the door marked solarium. They stepped inside to a row of floor-to-ceiling windows overlooking the patio they had passed on the way in and the same view that had caught their attention. A middle-aged woman in a light-green nurse's uniform hurried toward them from her station behind a short counter. Ellie could see only three residents in the large room, two dozing by the windows and the third studying the same faraway view she had admired only minutes ago. ''Are you the folks for Mr. Williams?'' the woman asked. Graham nodded. ''He's right over here.'' She led the way toward the man watching out the window. ''You'll have to speak up. He's a little hard of hearing. He's having a good day, though.'' She stepped around the man's wheelchair and looked him in the face. Her voice was noticeably louder when she spoke. ''Mr. Williams, you have visitors.''

''I do?'' His words were full of such surprise, so unaccustomed was he to the idea that anyone would stop to see him these days, and he tried to turn his head to see who these visitors might possibly be.

''I'll swing your chair around so you can be more comfortable chatting,'' the nurse said, as she positioned his wheelchair so he was facing them. She slid two straight chairs toward them, and they sat down in front of the old man. Ellie took her first good look at Mr. Williams and was surprised at what she saw. Instead of the wrinkled, shrunken man she was expecting, she saw a lean, sinewy gentleman in a blue workshirt, the sleeves rolled up to the elbow, and a pair of khaki work pants. He could easily pass for a man twenty years his junior. The skin was stretched tight on his face, defying any wrinkle to gain a foothold there. His eyes, a faded blue, were magnified behind strong lenses on wire-rim glasses, but she was glad to see an inquisitiveness in those eyes that hinted at the general alertness of the man. One glance at his large gnarled hands, resting on the arms of the chair, told a story of a life of hard work. He hadn't acquired such an angular physique through any lowfat diet or by running marathons. She had to smile at the unruly wisp of white hair defiantly coiled on the top of his head.

''Do I know you folks?'' he asked in a voice that didn't seem to fit his spare body. It was low-pitched and husky but a little breathless. ''My old brain ain't workin' like it used to.'' He tapped the top of his head with the knuckles of his right hand.

"No, you don't know us, Mr. Williams," Graham explained. "My name is Graham Stahmers and this is Ellie Regan. We're trying to find information about a man by the name of Jerome LeClaire. He was my grandfather. We thought you might have known him." Ellie watched the face closely for any sign of recognition.

"Jerome LeClaire, you say?" There was a vague look in his eyes, and Ellie decided that, sadly, they were probably wasting their time.

A glimmer of recognition came over him just then. "Oh, you mean Frenchy!"

"What's that, Mr. Williams?" Graham asked.

"That be the name folks called 'im. Frenchy LeClaire." He looked closely at Graham with renewed interest. "You be old Frenchy's boy, ya say?"

"His grandson, sir."

"Oh, yes, yes, that'd be the way of it, wouldn't it?" He shook his head. The memory of his old friend seemed to be troubling him. "Bad business. Bad, bad business."

"What's that, sir?" Graham asked.

The old man cocked his head and looked toward the ceiling. "I remember a baby boy and a little girl."

"My mother is Lucille."

He brightened. "Yes, yes, little Lucy. A cute little one, as I remember." He looked suddenly at Ellie and his eyes grew larger behind the glasses. "Ya say this one here's little Lucy all growed up?"

"No, no, this is Ellie Regan." The question had knocked Graham back in his chair. He was beginning to see he had a chore ahead of him to try to extract information from this man.

"Of course, of course, my brain ain't what it used to be." Again came the thump on the head.

"Sir, do you know what happened to the little boy? Lucille's brother?"

"No more'n a baby. Yep, just a baby. Somebody took him in. Who was it now? Good friend a mine." Thump. "Joe Rathburn. That's it. Joe and Hannah Rathburn. Nice folks, too.

Already had four of their own. Good people. Yep, good people.''

Ellie was taking notes in Graham's notepad. They had discussed taping the interview but feared that might unnerve the old gentleman. Graham went on. ''Mr. Williams, do you know if the Rathburns stayed around here, or did they move away?''

''Oh, they'd be long dead and gone by now.''

''I know, but did they live here or move somewhere else?''

''Last I heard old Joe took his brood off to Denver. That was years ago.''

Graham proceeded carefully. ''When I first mentioned my grandfather's name, you said 'bad business.' What did you mean by that?''

''T'was. Awful bad business. Blaine Whitiker killed him, ya know?''

''Blaine Whitiker killed my grandfather!?'' Graham spoke each word separately and carefully, and the old man's eyes widened at the reaction his words had on his visitor. He shifted uncomfortably in his wheelchair.

''Well, now don't be takin' me wrong, young fella. He weren't arrested nor nothin', but he done it all the same. Not so's you could throw him in jail, you understand, but he done it. Everybody round these parts says so.''

''What do you mean exactly?''

Graham had been priming the pump with his questions, and suddenly the story began to flow freely and with little prompting. The old man cradled his chin in one of the big hands propped on the arm of the chair. He fixed his eyes on a spot just over the heads of his visitors as he began. ''Ya see, him and old Frenchy started out the best of friends. That's why the whole business was so bad. They worked in the fields back in the thirties tryin' for the big strike. Always broke or near it. Frenchy was always the brain man in that there pair. I remember he headed out somewhere or the other raisin' money for what was supposed to be a sure strike. He'd have got it, too, if he coulda stayed with it. Told me his own self on his deathbed, what he regretted most.'' His eyes refocused suddenly on Graham. ''Except for them kids of his. They was his pride for sure. He blamed hisself that they was so bad off. But I remember he says to me, 'Elmer, I owe a lot a people, and I'll never be able to pay 'em back now.' That bothered him terrible.'' Ellie was shaking as she scribbled the words on her notepad, the words that tied her grandfather to the story. She was more than ready to forgive a man for whom she had harbored such bad feelings, and she knew her grandfather would, too.

The old man rubbed a rough hand over the top of his head and went on. ''The two of them fellers never had enough money. Almost made it at Buffalo Ridge, though.''

Graham leaned forward and interrupted. ''What about Buffalo Ridge?''

Elmer Williams focused on him as if he were seeing him for the first time. ''Buffalo Ridge? Now, that there was a real strike. Frenchy knowed they was oil there. Like I said, Frenchy was the brains of that bunch. Them two hit a well that paid out pretty good for a while, but they missed the gushers by maybe a quarter mile. Had the rights to some of that land but ran outta money before they hit the big 'un. That one well was payin some, not much. They was workin' it and diggin' coal up Maryville way. Workin' theirselves to a early grave is what we told 'em. Moved into town 'bout then when the Maryville mine give out. That's when they come up with that there tomfoolery 'bout the mountain.''

''You mean Mount Rushmore?'' Graham asked.

''Yup. Folks told Frenchy he was crazy. Had one leg shorter than the other. Musta been two or three inches. Limped bad. Army wouldn't mess with 'im on account of that there leg. I know that for a fact. Not that he didn't try hard enough after that Pearl Harbor business. Folks said he'd kill hisself up there on them presidents' heads, but he never did. Made good money too hangin' on them ropes, and them two poured every cent they got into that there oil field. Scrimped and saved, even from them little ones. Frenchy blamed hisself for that. Anyhow that's when it happened. Blame fools, drivin' back from that there mountain late at night and them dead tired from a day's work. Old Blaine fell asleep and drove off the road. Frenchy was hurt real bad. Almost died right then and there. Been better off if he did.''

''Why do you say that?''

Mr. Williams stared through Graham as if he hadn't heard the question. For a moment he looked every one of his ninety-plus years as his face darkened and his brow knit into a frown. ''Mighta turned out a sight better for Mary and them little ones. Somethin' happened to Blaine Whitiker after that night. Weren't hurt in the crash, not so's you'd know it anyways, but lots a folks in these parts said he musta hit his head or somethin'. He weren't the same after that. Stole the oil money from that there one well. Anyways that's what folks said. Oh, he did it clever-like so's no one knowed for sure. What could Frenchy do? He was flat in his bed fightin' for his life. Bled 'im dry, Blaine did, him and the kids. They was starvin', them little ones. Mary seen what she had to do. Sent the old one back somewhere East to a orphanage. The young'un she kept long as she could. Give 'im up after Frenchy died when she got so sick.''

''What happened to their oil well?''

The old man raised a hand a few inches off the handle of his wheelchair and gave a wave of dismissal. ''Oh, that purty near dried up. Then Blaine bought out Frenchy's half a Buffalo Ridge. Stole it if ya ask me. Frenchy needed the money bad for doctoring. He died and Mary followed not long after. She was tore up bad about them kids and Frenchy. You could see how she would be, can't ya?''

Graham nodded. The three sat in the bright sun streaming through the solarium windows. Ellie stole a look sideways at Graham. His face was ashen. Finally, he asked, ''What about Blaine Whitiker?''

The old man's face twisted into a strange smile. ''That pole-cat? People treated him like he was some kind a prairie rattler. Kept their distance if ya know what I mean. Better'n he deserved. Never did get the big gusher. Couldn't scrape together enough money to go deep as he shoulda. He sold out what he had in Buffalo Ridge, after the war if I remember rightly.'' Mr. Williams raised his hand and scratched his chin. ''Lassiter bought it out. Like they bought out every wildcatter what couldn't sink his own well. Whitiker moved outta here, somewhere west I'm thinkin'. Folks hereabouts said good riddance to 'im, too. Lassiter brought in some good wells on that same land. People round here laughed about that. Not 'cause of Frenchy LeClaire, ya understand,'' he added quickly. "But they was happy old Blaine Whitiker never made no money from the bad he done a good man.''

Graham leaned forward and studied the old man closely. "Mr. Williams, what were my grandparents like?''

The old fellow rubbed a hand across the stubble on his chin. "They was good folks. To his dying breath old Frenchy regretted what become of his wife and little ones. If he coulda done anythin' to help 'em he'd a done it in a minute. That and the money he'd borrowed for the field. He hated to be beholden. Told me that his own self. Hated to die beholden like that." His eyes got a faraway look in them. "Frenchy was a good friend to lots a people round here. Me? I always knowed we let 'im down. He wouldn't have let us down like we done to him. Ya know what I mean? And that's somethin' I'll carry to my grave. We was scrabbling to stay ahead ourselves and didn't have much to help with what with the mine closin' up at Maryville and such. I'm not makin' excuses, ya understand. We shoulda done more. But folks round here didn't know how bad things was with 'em and that's the truth.'' Ellie saw the gnarled hands grip the handles of the chair. "Folks done more for Mary, you understand, but it was too late for that one. Her heart was broke clean in two. Folks come from miles around to their funerals. Not that it was goin' to do 'em any good then. Too late if ya know what I mean.'' Almost as an afterthought, he added, "You'd have liked the pair of 'em if you'd knowed 'em. Good folks.''

Graham reached across and patted one of the old man's hands. "I'm sure I would have, Mr. Williams. And thanks to you, I feel like I almost do know them. Now I think we've taken up about enough of your time.''

The old man let out a short laugh which brought on a hacking cough. After he recovered, he said, "All I got's time, ya know. And all I got up here is old stuff.'' There went another thump on his head. ''You young folks come back anytime to visit. I just sit out here most days and think about the good ol' days.'' That brought on an unexpected chuckle and another brief bout of coughing. ''Trouble was, them days didn't seem so good while I was a-livin' 'em,'' he managed finally. ''Now don't that beat all?''

Graham stood up and reached for the man's hand. They shook almost formally. ''Thanks again. I can't begin to tell you how much you've helped.''

The man waved him off. ''Don't mention it.''

Ellie stood and reached for the hand. Her own hand disappeared in the gnarled one he produced, and his grip was firm, almost too much so. She leaned over and planted a kiss on the top of his head. ''Thanks,'' she said quietly.

Elmer Williams beamed. ''Bring this little one here back with ya. She's a beauty. The spittin' image of her grandma, I can tell ya. The very spittin' image.''

Ellie laughed at the man's confusion about her parentage, realizing there was little reason to correct his mistake. He had linked her unwittingly to the participants of his story, and what was the harm in that? she asked herself. She and Graham walked to the door, nodded to the nurse still on duty, and Ellie turned for one last look at Elmer Williams as he sat by the windows. He was watching them, and she gave him a wave which he returned with a smile.

''What a nice man,'' Ellie said as the two retraced their steps down the hall to the front door.

''And such a fountain of information,'' Graham added. ''That head of his is just full to the top with the past, isn't it?'' She could tell by the tone of his voice that he was excited about all he'd learned. Once back in the car, he turned to her. ''So what do think? Did you get all your questions answered? I noticed you didn't say much.''

''Remember, we agreed you were going to do all the talking,'' she said with just a trace of irritation. ''I thought it went very well. It was less confusing for him that way. So the real question is did you get all the answers you wanted?''

"I think so. I'll probably remember something later I should have asked him, but no, I think I found out what I wanted to know. And you got it all down?"

"Right here." She produced the notepad. "But you'd better let me go over what I wrote to make sure it makes sense. I was writing as fast as I could."

"I've got a lot to tell Mom. Who were the people who took my uncle in? It was Rathburn, wasn't it?"

"Right." She consulted the notebook. "Joe Rathburn."

"I wonder if he knows he was adopted? Do you suppose they told him?" He was talking more to himself than to her. "Even if they did, later, he wouldn't know how to trace anyone since my mother had taken a different name. And anyway they might not have told him. People back then lots of times didn't."

"Look him up on the Internet," Ellie said. "People find relatives all the time that way."

"If I could find him, my mom would go through the roof."

Ellie smiled. "I wish you luck. That would be the real topping to this whole story, wouldn't it?" She felt a little strange when she said it. It was almost as if she were beginning to put an end to all the excitement she had had over the past several days. She couldn't believe it had been days and not years.

"We need to celebrate," he said as he started the car. "What do you say to dinner?"

"Sounds fine, but I need to change. I'm a mess after our little stint in that dusty library."

He glanced at his watch. "It's four-thirty now. How does seven o'clock sound to you?"

"Perfect."

He aimed the car in the direction of town and let his brain engage. Something was happening to him, putting him in the most dejected of moods. He should have been "out-of-his-mind" happy at the moment, he told himself, but he wasn't. Oh, he was satisfied, no, more than satisfied, with what he'd found out about his grandparents and all but why then this

disquieting weight that had settled in his chest. Finding out
firsthand all the sad details of their lives as he just had—that
was bound to be sobering, he reminded himself. That had to
be it. He pulled into the Pine Rest parking lot and up to Ellie's
door. She turned to him before she got out. ''You okay?''

''Sure, I'm fine. Why?''

''You haven't said one word since we left the home.''

He forced a smile. ''Sorry. Guess finding out all that stuff
affected me more than I thought.''

Remembering her own feelings while sitting in her car in
front of the remains of her grandparents' farmstead, she understood. ''Do you want to talk about it?''

''No, I'll be fine. I just have a few things to think over.''

''You're sure.''

''I'm sure. Seven tonight?''

''Right.'' She smiled at him and hopped out.

As he drove across town to his own motel, he had no luck
chasing the depressing feeling. He let himself into his room,
flopped heavily on the bed, put his hands beneath his head,
and stared up at the ceiling. He would force himself to think
things out clearly. Who was he trying to kid, anyway? He
knew what the trouble was, and what he'd learned this afternoon from Elmer Williams hadn't caused it, oh, maybe it had
a little but not much. No, the real reason he was feeling the
way he was had everything to do with Ellie Regan and what
he knew he would tell her tonight—had to tell her. After all,
he was through here, wasn't he? He would move on to Rapid
City for a day, maybe two, to finish his research and then it
was back to Chicago to get serious about the *Tribune* article.
The deadline was looming. And he was already thinking about
the piece for *The New Yorker*; it was beginning to push its
way into the front of his brain the way articles did when they
seemed to demand to be written. One thing for sure, it would
definitely take all of the creativity he could manage.

The thought that he would soon have to say good-bye to
Ellie had been playing at the corners of his mind for at least
the last twenty-four hours, and he was angry at himself for

making it that important. After all, they'd known each other all of three days, he reminded himself. He thought then, as he had many times over the last three days, about the extraordinary coincidence of meeting this woman at this time at this place, both looking for the same long-dead person but for totally different reasons. More like two hundred million to one, he decided, and he took a deep breath and let it out slowly. *Is that what they call fate? C'mon, you don't believe in stuff like that,* he reminded himself. Sure, he'd been attracted to her. She was beautiful. It was great to be with her. They'd been a team after all. He shook his head cradled by his hands at that idea. *A team! That's a good one. If it hadn't been for her, I would've cleared out of here the first day. I wouldn't have found out a single thing. She forced me to stay with it.* He sat up suddenly. *Now wait a minute. I don't have time for all this,* he said to himself. *Anyway, what kind of a life do I have to offer? I'm never home.* The thought of the editor's position he'd been offered just weeks ago drifted into his head just then, but he pushed it aside. He'd been down this road before and frankly, the thought of settling down frightened him more than a little.

This wasn't the first time Graham had had such a conversation with himself, but it was the first time the object of his conversation had ever meant so much. Ellie was different from anyone he'd ever known. He knew he had never in his life felt this way about any woman. She was beautiful, bright, fun, clever, witty, thoughtful, understanding. . . . He was mentally ticking off her obvious traits almost as if he were trying to tip some invisible scales. He stood and began pacing in the tiny room letting the thoughts tumble in his brain. *Aren't you forgetting one little thing? No, on second thought, you're forgetting two things. First, you really don't know whether she feels even remotely the same way about you, and, second, you've known her all of three days. Three days!* That fresh thought seemed to weigh in heavily on the side of common sense or what he chose to consider as common sense. *Remember what you think about love at first sight? And three days comes pretty darn close to first sight.* But the mere thought of the word love made him sit again and bury his head in his hands. *Why'd you have to bring that into it? I'm totally clueless as far as love is concerned.*

Promptly at 7:00 he pulled into the Pine Rest parking lot next to Ellie's Toyota. He'd made up his mind. He was finally seeing things rightheaded or so he thought. He'd put away all those emotions that had gotten him so confused in the first place. She stepped out of her room just then at the sight of his car. She was wearing a powder blue dress with a scoop neck, and he felt the weight in his chest again at the sight of her and had serious second thoughts about the words he had rehearsed on the way here.

"Hi," she said brightly as she opened the door and climbed in next to him. Graham returned her greeting and smiled, but there was a decided coolness about him. It was a continuation of the mood she'd sensed on the way back from Elk Creek this afternoon. She thought then he was still digesting the words of the old friend of his grandfather. Now she wasn't so sure. She was on her guard. They struggled with conversation on the way to the restaurant, something that had never been a problem over the last three days. Graham had picked a new spot, Danny's, not far from downtown, and they were led to a table near a noisy party celebrating a birthday.

A fidgety waitress took their order. Ellie guessed this might be her first night, and she became convinced of it when the girl made little pretense about studying the menu over Graham's shoulder to get their orders right. Ellie thought he might be amused at such bumbling but he seemed not to even notice or at least chose not to notice. After the girl had gone, Ellie toyed with her water glass. She didn't know it, but things were about to go from bad to worse. She started out innocently enough covering some of the ground from the afternoon. "So have you thought any more about finding your uncle?"

With his forefinger Graham was tracing the checked pattern of the tablecloth in front of him. "I'll try but it looks hopeless. All I've got is a possible name. I can't even be sure he kept the same first name."

Ellie didn't like the lifeless tone in his voice. "It's worth a try," she insisted. "You can't tell how common that name is. Start with Denver. That's where Mr. Williams said the family went from here and, who knows, they might have stayed."

"I'll do that."

His tone, intentional or not she couldn't tell, definitely hinted at the obviousness of her suggestion, and she felt the heat rise to her cheeks. "What's wrong with you tonight?"

He'd gone back to his tablecloth tracing and looked up at her question knowing she'd provided a perfect opening for the clean separation he'd decided on, but he didn't want to spoil their dinner. "Nothing. Why?"

"I just made a reasonable suggestion, and you act like I'm some kind of idiot."

"I said I'd do it, didn't I?"

"But the way you said it. Like you were humoring me. I hate to be humored."

"Sorry."

"There you did it again."

This time he *was* confused. "Did what again?"

"You said sorry, but you sure didn't mean it."

"How can you tell me what I meant? I meant what I said. I'm sorry if I offended you."

Miss Fidgety showed up just then with their salads, putting an end to their wordplay at least for the time being. They each picked at the contents on the plates in front of them. To Ellie the pieces of lettuce might as well have been pieces of cardboard. She pushed her salad away half-eaten, determined to get to the heart of things. She was pretty sure what was coming and decided there was little reason to mince words. "Now what?" she asked.

Graham looked up at the ambiguous question. "Pardon me?"

"Now what?" she repeated.

He chose to take her question literally. "I plan to head back to Rapid City tomorrow for a little more research and then back home."

She was glaring at him. "You know what I mean."

''No, I'm afraid I don't. Apparently I don't have your mind-reading powers.''

''Shall we exchange phone numbers and addresses and promise to write every week until school starts?'' Now it was her voice that had taken on a tone. ''That's what we used to do at camp. Didn't you ever go to camp?'' Ellie's voice had climbed a decibel or two, and the folks celebrating at the long table next door had grown suddenly quiet as they watched the gathering storm.

''Let's not get carried away here,'' Graham was saying. ''We've had a good three days. Can't we be friends?''

''And this is the way you treat friends?'' It wasn't necessary for the group at the next table to strain to hear this question. ''You've been acting like a real pain since this afternoon and I finally figured out why. But you don't need to worry, Mr. Stahmers. I have absolutely no intention of chasing you all the way back to Chicago if that's what's worrying you.''

''Did I say that?''

''You didn't have to. It's written all over your face. But don't flatter yourself. I got along just fine before I met you, and I assure you I'll get along just fine after you leave.'' Miss Fidgety chose the worst possible moment to arrive with their entrees, and Ellie stood up suddenly in front of the shocked young woman who was doing her best to balance a fully loaded tray over her right shoulder on the palm of one hand. ''Give mine to him,'' Ellie said, pointing at Graham across the table.

This was too much for the girl with the tray, and she only narrowly averted the disaster she'd already had nightmares about by managing to transfer the tray of food to the very edge of the table where she was balancing it precariously. ''Is there a problem, ma'am?'' she pleaded, certain she faced being fired on the spot for doing what she hadn't a clue. ''Something wrong with the salad?''

Ellie was almost to the front door by this time, and Graham was chasing after her leaving the waitress near tears with two dinners and no one to serve them to. The group at the next table was exchanging looks.

By the time Graham got outside Ellie was already to the sidewalk heading in the direction of her motel which was at least a two-mile walk. "Wait a minute," he called and she hesitated. He trotted up beside her. "What's gotten into you? You can't walk all the way back to the motel. It's miles."

"Wanna bet?" She started off again.

"Calm down," he tried in a coaxing tone.

She stopped again. "You'd better get back to your dinner."

"I'm not going back without you."

"Well, it looks like neither one of us is going anywhere, because I'm not going back," she declared.

"I still don't know what you're so upset about. What did I say that made you so mad?"

She glared at him. "I find it hard to believe you don't know, but I'll spell it out for you. You manufactured a complete personality change since this afternoon. It started just after we left the home." She set her jaw. "Oh, don't look at me like that. You know it's true. And I know why too. It took me long enough, but I figured it out in there." She pointed toward the door of Danny's. "You got scared. That's right. Scared because you thought we were getting too serious. And don't try to deny it."

"I didn't say anything."

"You'd better not. What makes you think I was getting serious, anyway?"

"Listen," Graham said, "we need to talk this over. You won't go back in?" She shook her head. "That's okay. That's perfectly all right. I don't feel hungry myself now either. You wait right here until I go back and pay the bill. Then we'll go somewhere and talk. Okay?" She said nothing. He moved a few steps away and turned. "Don't move from that spot. I'll be right back." He disappeared through the door and went back to the table. His steak and her chicken entrees were waiting at their places. The party at the next table fell quiet again when they saw him. They were ready for the next episode. He stood by the table scanning the back of the restaurant until he spotted their waitress. He intercepted her as she was about to deliver a glass of wine, and she nearly dropped the glass when she saw him.

"Oh, sir, is something the matter? Is the lady not feeling well? Is it something I did?"

"No, everything's fine," he assured her. "Something came up, that's all. Could I have my check?"

"Oh, certainly, sir." She set the wine down hurriedly and pawed through the checks in her apron pocket until she came upon his. "Sir, would you like me to box those dinners? Wouldn't take me a minute."

He snatched the ticket. "No thanks." He hurried to the cashier near the door and slipped the check along with his credit card on the glass in front of her. "I'm in kind of a hurry."

"Of course, sir. Was everything satisfactory for you this evening?"

"Couldn't be better," he answered and remembered that was the tone that had gotten him into all the trouble in the first place. He waited impatiently as his card cleared approval, signed the printout with a generous tip for the girl they had worried to an early grave, and hurried out the front door just in time to see Ellie climbing into a cab by the curb. He looked up into the clear evening Wyoming sky. "I didn't even know they had a taxi in this place," he said to anyone who cared to hear.

Chapter Ten

Ellie couldn't believe her eyes when she spotted, rattling down the street, the orange and black sedan with *taxi* emblazoned in black letters across its side and a lighted strip crowning its top, but she recovered soon enough to wave it to a stop. Under normal circumstances she might have thought twice about climbing into such a strange excuse for a cab with a wild-haired driver in a Hawaiian shirt in a strange town, but at this moment she was grateful for the deliverance it provided. The tears held off until she had given her destination and had dropped back into the dark, cavernous back seat of the old Chevrolet, but then they came in torrents.

The driver was keeping such close tabs on his passenger's condition through the rearview mirror that he had to lean hard on his brakes to avoid rear-ending a truck stopped for a red-light. Ellie hardly noticed the panic stop. She was already moving beyond the release of a good cry and was caught somewhere between fury and heartache at the moment with little time for mundane traffic problems. She couldn't decide if she were more angry with herself or with Graham. By the time the cab had pulled into the Pine Rest parking lot, she had worked up to a fairly serious rage over the way out Graham had chosen for himself. Instead of being straightforward with her about the way he really felt, he was going to try to scare her away with some phony mood swing. As if she weren't smart enough to see through that. But why the nagging irritation with herself? She knew what her roommate would say when they talked all this over back home: she'd led with her heart. Erin liked to say things like that. She gritted her teeth at the truth of it. She'd led him around by the hand for the past three days helping him find his family. And for what? She pulled a fresh tissue from her purse as the tears began again. What really hurt is she really liked the guy. She'd even allowed herself to daydream about the blossoming of a romance. It would have to be long distance for sure, but Chicago and Dubuque weren't really all that far apart.

"I said that'll be two and a quarter."

Ellie jerked forward in the seat. "Excuse me?"

"The fare, lady. You said Pine Rest, didn't ya? That's two and a quarter."

"Oh, of course. I'm sorry." She dug in her purse and pulled out a five. "Here," she said as she handed it to him and climbed out of the backseat. She slammed the door and marched stoically toward her room.

"Hey, thanks a lot, lady," the Hawaiian shirt called through the open window as he dropped the car into gear and squealed toward the exit.

If Lil hadn't already gone home after her day's work, she would have seen Graham's car pass by the Pine Rest Motel exactly six times. Three times heading south and three times heading north. On the third pass going north, he nearly stopped. He slowed at the entrance, saw Ellie's car and the light in the window of her room as he had on each of the previous five trips, but at the last minute he sped up and went right on by like before. But this he time didn't turn around at the Convenience Store a block down the street but instead drove straight to his motel across town. There was a fast-food restaurant near his motel, and, convinced he was hungry, he pulled through the carry-out lane to pick up a burger and fries. Back in his room he sat down to eat only to find he wasn't nearly as hungry as he'd thought.

He tried to watch some television but found himself pacing the floor mulling over the deplorable way he'd botched things.

Not lost on him was the fact that the split he had intended when he went out the door tonight had, in fact, been accomplished. It had been a good deal messier than he would have liked, but the whole thing was over. Except now he wasn't certain that's what he really wanted at all. Around 11:00 he finally reached a simple conclusion: he needed to apologize. In fact, he was convinced he had made a terrible mistake. He climbed in the car and headed across town again to the Pine Rest rehearsing what he would say. He pulled into the lot, saw that Ellie's window was dark, drove right out again, and headed back the way he'd come. He put in a miserable night of tossing and turning, aware of each hour on the luminous clock dial by his bed. He fell into a deep sleep for the first time all night just before 6:00 and awoke with a start. It was 8:20. "Darn!" he shouted as he scrambled out of bed and grabbed for his clothes. He'd planned to see Ellie before she left. To apologize. It was the least he could do for what had happened last night. And maybe if he apologized . . . well, he didn't know. Now he wondered if he might be too late.

Ellie was up just after 7:00. She showered, dressed, and packed, then hauled her suitcases to the car. As she tucked the last of her belongings into the trunk, she saw Lil pull in and nose her car next to the office for the start of her day. Ellie checked her watch. She decided to grab a quick breakfast before starting out. If there was room for it, that is, beside the five-pound rock already resting uncomfortably in her stomach. She walked through the door of the tiny dining room to see Lil pouring herself a cup of coffee. The perceptive little woman eyed her young friend from head to toe before drawling, "Well, if you don't look a sight!"

"Lil, I'm not in the mood."

Lil could see which way the wind was blowing today, and she knew enough to tread lightly, but she by no means had any intention of giving up on her matchmaking. "A nice hot cup of joe and one a them delicious long johns, and you'll be good as new."

"By all means," Ellie said as she reached for one of the

frosted beauties. ''I've only gained fifteen pounds, and I swore I wouldn't go home until I hit twenty.''

Lil clicked her tongue. ''Listen to you now. Are we feelin' a little sorry for ourselves today?''

Ellie smiled sheepishly as she poured a cup of coffee. ''Well, maybe just a little.''

''And it's that Chicago fella, what's causin' all this here trouble, is it?''

''He makes me so mad! He was running away as hard as he could last night, and I wasn't even chasing.''

''Uh-huh,'' Lil said with a roll of the eyes for no one to see. She was certain she'd seen signs of chasing on both sides in the last three days. ''And were ya thinkin' about maybe doin' some chasin'?''

Ellie was sitting at one of the tables now sipping her coffee though the long john was still untouched on a paper plate in front of her. Her face reddened slightly at Lil's suggestion. ''The thought had crossed my mind. I know we hadn't known each other for very long,'' she added quickly, ''but we'd been through quite a bit together, what with finding out about his grandparents and all, and I thought, well, you know, I thought I could see some kind of spark there.'' Her voice trailed off, and she fumbled for a tissue in her purse hanging on the chair next to her.

Lil watched her and pursed her lips in thought. ''Ya like this feller quite a bit, don't ya?''

''Maybe I do. Oh, I don't know.'' She looked up suddenly with fire in her eyes. ''When I think of last night, it makes me so mad I could chew nails. You should have seen him, Lil. He was scared to death. You could see it in his eyes. I don't know what he thought. That I was going to drag him off against his will or something.''

''Men!'' Lil said with an inflection that was intended to explain the whole mystery of the opposite sex in that one simple word.

''You can say that again!'' Ellie said. She'd obviously heard and understood fully everything Lil was trying to say.

''But they can be a tricky bunch to figure out,'' Lil went

on. "Sometimes they run the hardest and the fastest when they're feelin' the most like not runnin'."

"That sounds stupid."

"Sounds stupid to me, too, but ya gotta remember who you're dealin' with here. Maybe it's cause they've been used to runnin' all the time. Or maybe they just need somebody to explain why runnin's not such a good idea."

Ellie smiled at this homespun philosophy and took a bite of her long john. She thought over what Lil had said as she chewed and swallowed. "You may be right, but I wonder if some men just don't want to ever stop running."

"Could be. But I always thought them kind wasn't worth worryin' about."

"And how do I find out which kind he is?"

"Just don't be in such a hurry to start runnin' off yourself."

Ellie was a little irritated at what Lil seemed to be saying, that she should sit around waiting for Graham to decide what he was going to do. "Lil, I've never been the shrinking violet type. He knows where I live. If he's interested, he can find me. Not that that's ever going to happen if last night was any indication."

"Ya never can tell. But one last piece of advice from an old woman and then I'll shut my trap. If he does come around, don't treat him like some dog what stayed out all night. Meet the feller halfway. Promise?"

Ellie smiled at the strange advice. "Promise."

"Good. Now I suppose you'll be leavin' again if I catch the drift."

"Right. I'm going back to Rapid City. I still haven't done a cave yet."

The woman's eyes brightened. "A cave, is it? Cathedral Cave is the one." She went scurrying to the office area and her rack of travel folders and hurried back with a colorful one. "Now, have ya a place to stay?"

"Well, no. Is that a problem?"

"This is the busy season, mind ya? I'd be happy ta call a friend at a lovely place. Black Hills Motor Lodge, it is. Would ya like me ta do that for ya?"

Ellie nodded. "If you think it's best, sure, go ahead."

"Better safe than sorry. You just settle there and have another cup a that delicious coffee. I'll fix it all for ya. Margaret's her name. Margaret Connely. Lovely lady. She'll treat ya right." Lil disappeared through the door, and Ellie heard her on the telephone shortly making arrangements. She took the woman's advice and poured a second cup of coffee. She was feeling some better. In a matter of minutes Lil was back. "It's all fixed for ya. And it's a lucky thing. She had only one room left and the vacancy signs are up all along her street. Now I'll write directions on this folder here." She held up the Cathedral Cave folder. "If she don't treat you right, report it direct to me."

Ellie smiled. "I'll do that but I'm sure everything will be fine." She finished her coffee and the rest of the long john and said good-bye to Lil, more than a little reluctantly. She had become attached to the woman who seemed to want to put up such a hard front, but Ellie guessed that was to hide such a kind heart.

"Now, promise old Lil one thing," she said as she walked to the door with her new, young friend. "If you and Mr. Chicago ever do get together, you let me know about it. You hear?"

"I promise. But I wouldn't be holding my breath 'til that happens," Ellie informed her and did her best to smile.

"Oh, ya never can tell. No, ya never can tell."

It couldn't have been more than thirty minutes later, Lil was sitting on her high stool by the counter in the office paging idly through the latest issue of *Innkeepers Monthly* when a familiar car swung into the parking lot. Lil barely looked up, but she noticed the car all the same. Her faint smile was enough to give that away. After all, she'd been expecting him. But, even though she would never admit it to a living soul, she had become just the tiniest bit nervous because he was taking his own sweet time. She gave him just a glance as he came through the door and smiled again. It was in the bag, she knew from the looks of him. His hair was disheveled, his eyes bloodshot, he hadn't shaved. He looks worse than she does, Lil decided in that one quick glance. "What can I do for you?" she asked, sliding her magazine aside.

"Hello, I was here the other morning looking for Ellie Regan."

Lil feigned sudden recognition. "You're that friend of hers from Chicago. Now I remember. You was lookin' for her other day, and I sent ya to the Pantry. Did ya catch up with her there?"

"Yes, I did. Thank you. Is she here today by chance?"

Lil ignored the question. "What a nice young thing that one is! Wouldn't you say?"

"Yes, she most certainly is. Have you seen her this morning?"

"I says to myself when I sees that one, I says, 'Lil, how's that pretty one kept from being snapped up?' You'd have thought somebody woulda married up with her long ago. Wouldn't ya have thought that, Mr.—?"

"Stahmers," he answered for her.

"Oh, yes, Mr. Stahmers. Ellie speaks so highly of ya. You and that grandfather of yours."

Graham's eyebrows arched at that news. "Really?"

"Oh, yes, Mr. Stahmers, she like to wear my ears out with her talkin' on ya." Her face clouded dramatically. "Except for this mornin', you know. She was kinda outta sorts with ya this mornin'."

Graham nodded uncomfortably at this news. "That's why I'm here. To try to set things straight."

"Ah, what a good thing for ya to be doin', to set things straight like ya said. But ya just missed her. Left down that road out there not more'n thirty minutes ago."

His face showed his disappointment. "That's what I was afraid of. But you see I overslept. I wanted to get here before she left." He had fallen under the power of Lil's questioning eyes and seemed bent on telling everything. "You see, I tried to come over here last night, but—" he drew the line at recalling for this woman his many trips past the place—"I . . . didn't make it."

"Lost your courage?" she asked gravely.

"Something like that."

Lil clicked her tongue. "What a pity ya missed her. The dear girl: I'm certain she'd a loved to hear what ya had to say."

"Did she happen to mention if she was going straight home? I mean to Dubuque?"

Lil looked at the ceiling above her and tapped on her chin with a forefinger. "Now, let me see. I'm certain she said she was stoppin' in Rapid City. Oh, yes, now I remember, she was goin' to try to get in at the Black Hills Motor Lodge, that's it. I'll write directions if ya want to look her up there." She scurried to her rack of folders, came back with the colorful Cathedral Cave one, and busied herself scribbling the best way to her friend Margaret Connely's place. "There, that'll get ya to the door." She handed the brochure across to him.

"Thanks a lot." He stood for a moment deciphering her scribbles, and she took the opportunity to trap his right hand, resting on the counter, with her own. He looked at her in surprise.

"When ya talk to her, tell her somethin' for old Lil, somethin' we was discussin' just this mornin'."

"Sure, what's that?"

"Just tell her runnin's bad for her."

"Running's bad? I'm afraid I don't agree, but I'll tell her what you said."

"Oh, you're a runner, too?"

"I get serious about it from time to time."

"Then I'll tell you too. Runnin's bad for ya."

He shrugged, unwilling to get involved in the merits of exercise with this woman, recovered his hand from under hers, and made for the door. "Thanks for your help."

"Don't mention it," Lil said, a hint of smile on her lips, as she eased back onto the stool and reached for the telephone.

Graham drove straight to his motel to put himself in better order for the day now that he had hopes of intercepting Ellie. He was moving on, himself, as he'd already told her, and after a shower and a much-needed shave, he packed and checked out. On the drive back to Rapid City he remembered every sight they'd shared on their earlier trip and almost every word she'd spoken. Or so he was convinced, at least. He rehearsed in his head what he planned to say to her. As he drew closer to the city, he gave Lil's directions a quick look. He'd tossed the folder on the seat next to him. Her writing, though a little shaky on the paper, was understandable enough, and he drove straight to the Black Hills Motor Lodge. As he pulled into the parking lot, he noticed the No Vacancy sign. Maybe she wasn't able to get in, he thought. He scanned the few cars there at this time of day for her familiar Toyota but was disappointed when he didn't see it. He hopped out and headed for the office located behind a pull-through at the center of the two-story building. A graying, heavyset woman was doing a crossword puzzle at the counter and looked up with a warm smile when he entered. "Good morning, may I help you?"

"Good morning," he answered. "I'm looking for someone who may be staying here. Ellie Regan?"

The woman's smile was so quick he didn't notice it. She'd been expecting him. "Why, yes, Miss Regan checked in with us this morning. I think she's out, though. Would you like me to ring her room to check for sure?"

Graham was relieved. "Please. Would you?"

"Of course." She picked up the house phone, dialed a number, and waited. After listening to six rings, she hung it up again. "I'm sorry, she is out. Would you like to leave a message?"

Graham stood undecided. He didn't know where he would be staying himself. He wasn't even sure how she was going to react to any kind of message from him. He was certain his best chance was to see her face-to-face. "No, I guess not. I'll stop back."

The woman smiled her understanding and watched him, her curiosity mounting, as he walked back to his car. He cruised the busy streets until he spotted a decent-looking motel with a vacancy sign. He checked in and unloaded his car. He sat on the edge of the bed trying to decide what to do next. He could call back to the Black Hills hotel and leave a message

that he was here and wanted to talk. But that didn't satisfy
him. He still thought he should give his message in person.
His glance rested on the folder with Lil's handwritten directions. He'd dropped it on the desk as he'd come in. *Cathedral
Cave,* he thought. *You don't suppose . . . She did say she
wanted to visit a cave.* He picked it up and looked at the
picture of the colorful rock formations shown on the front.
There was a map on the back, and he studied it, getting his
bearings. *Why not?* he decided.

As luck would have it, the street out front was one of the
ones clearly marked on the map, and he found the cave easily
after a ten-minute drive. His heart skipped a beat when he saw
the Toyota with Iowa plates among the cars in the lot. He got
out and looked around. Anyone expecting a gaping cave hole
in the side of a mountain would be disappointed at what they
saw here, he decided. Instead he saw a good-sized frame
building with a sign over the entrance in bold red lettering
announcing: CAVE ENTER HERE with an arrow pointing straight
down at the door. Graham went in. A few people were brows-
ing counters loaded with souvenirs, some dealing with rocks
and geology but most about the Black Hills in general. A sign
at a cash register read: CAVE TICKETS HERE. People seemed to
be queuing toward the back. He asked the girl behind the
counter, ''Is there a tour going?''

''Just leaving, but you can still catch it if you hurry.''

He paid his money, got his ticket, and joined the others
moving toward the twenty or so already crowding around a
solid gray door where a young woman in a khaki uniform was
just raising her flashlight to get everyone's attention. ''Stay
close together,'' she was saying, ''and watch your footing on
the stairs.'' She swung the door open revealing a rough stone
opening, the kind you would expect to see in a mine shaft,
and there were gasps from some of the ticketholders, the claus-
trophobics in the crowd, Graham guessed with a grin. What
did they expect? he wondered. It was a cave. He was at the
end of the line, and he watched closely as the first visitors
passed through the opening and descended out of sight. There
she was! Maybe the fifth or sixth through the door. He rec-

ognized the back of her head, her dark hair, short and gently curled. He almost shouted her name. *Now what?* he wondered. *How am I going to talk to her down there?* He followed the crowd down the wooden stairs beneath the naked light bulbs hanging from the rough, stone ceiling by metal conduit.

Once at the bottom he followed the stragglers down a narrow tunnel which opened suddenly into a cavern about fifteen feet across and twenty feet or so long. The group had formed a semicircle around the guide, and she had already started her explanation about stalactites and stalagmites. There was a tiny forest of the formations just behind her, the icicle-like wedges of limestone reaching from the chamber's ceiling to try to touch their counterparts jutting up from the floor. The crowd, including Ellie, close to the front, was engrossed in the young guide's words. Graham edged slowly along the fringe of people until he was behind Ellie but one row back.

The guide finished. "Follow me and watch your heads." Graham reached over the shoulder of the man in front of him as the crowd broke ranks and tapped Ellie on the shoulder. She spun around to glare at the man behind her who shrugged his shoulders in innocence and yanked a thumb toward his shoulder. "Not me, lady."

She adjusted her eyes and brought Graham's grinning face into focus. "Hi," he greeted her with a sheepish look.

Her jaw gaped in surprise. "What are *you* doing here?" She wasn't smiling.

"I need to talk to you."

"How did you find me?"

"It's a long story." The few remaining cave explorers were filing past them.

"Well? So what *are* you doing here?"

"I need to talk to you," he repeated himself.

"You already said that."

"This wasn't going the way he'd planned. He'd hoped for some help from her, but all he was getting was that stony look. What he said next just slipped out, a stab at something that might make her smile. "I've got a message for you from Lil." As soon as he said them, he realized how absurd the words sounded. Why would he chase after her all the way to Rapid City just to deliver a message from Lil?

Ellie was wondering exactly the same thing, but through some miracle of communication she managed to say it all with just one word. "Lil?!"

Knowing that all had been lost anyway, what was left to do but give her the message. "I know it doesn't make any sense, but she said to tell you running is bad for you."

Instead of the blank look he was expecting, he received the most beautiful smile, the best gift he could imagine in return for chasing her to the bottom of a cave. "She didn't by any chance suggest the same thing for you?" Ellie asked, still smiling.

"As a matter of fact she did."

"Good old Lil."

He still didn't know what the message meant, but the ice had broken just enough for him to launch into his little speech. It didn't go exactly as he'd planned but pretty much. "I'm sorry," he began and that was a good way to start. "You were right, I *was* trying to freeze you out last night. I know we've only known each other three days, four if you count today, but there's something going on here that I've never felt before. At least there is for me." He was anticipating any arguments from her, not knowing such words weren't necessary. "I know, I know, we live quite a ways apart. I've thought of that, but it's not that far really." This is where his tongue began to seem too large for his mouth. He felt like a schoolboy, and he hadn't felt like that in a long time. "I mean I'd like to see you. I mean I'd like to see you a lot more, and well, maybe . . . well, I don't know." The look he gave her was one of panic. "Now, if you don't feel the same way, just say so, and I'll try to find my way out of this place." He looked about him suddenly at the dripping limestone walls around them. "And I'll never bother you again, I promise."

Ellie had just the hint of a smile on her face. "Uh, last night would you say maybe you were getting ready for a little footrace?"

He was waiting for an answer, and she was asking questions. He was confused. "I don't know what you mean." Suddenly his eyes widened in understanding. "You mean . . . ?"

She nodded. "Uh-huh."

"Lil? That's what she was getting at?"

"Right again."

"But the message she gave was for you."

"And you," she reminded him.

"So how did she know I needed it?"

"Wellll." Her tone was an admission. "I might have mentioned it."

Her confession didn't phase him she was glad to see. "I'm the one who was running for the hills," he said. "But why did you get the message?"

"This is getting complicated. I guess she was afraid I wouldn't give you a chance to have your say. I have been known to let my temper get away from me sometimes." He was smiling. "I know, I know," she went on, "that is pretty hard to believe, but Lil must have been worried about it."

"Lil is a very smart lady," Graham said with a grin. "So will you?"

"Will I what?"

"Give me a chance?"

"Oh, yes!" she said with all the warmth she could manage.

He reached for her and pulled her close. Their lips met in the kiss Ellie knew she had been longing for since the day when they had sat together in the shadow of Devils Tower. She held tightly to him wondering how close she had come to losing him entirely.

"What are you two doing!?" Startled by the question echoing as it was off the cavern walls, the two parted and turned to stare at the intruder. It was their young guide in the khaki uniform bristling now with her authority. It wasn't lost on Ellie that the girl was probably not much older than the students in her high school. "If you can't keep up with the group, I'll call for someone to escort you out," the young woman snapped. She patted a walkie-talkie attached to her belt. "Don't you know you could get lost down here?"

Graham glanced quickly at Ellie with a look that said getting lost down here with her wouldn't be all that bad, but he turned a contrite face toward the young guide. ''Sorry.'' They followed her back out and down the tunnel not more than twenty feet into a much larger cavern. The curious eyes of the others on the tour watched the return of the pair who had been discovered lost by the guide's headcount.

The young woman stepped toward a box on the wall. ''Now, stay close together. I'm going to turn off the lights, and I want you to look toward the ceiling. You'll see the calcite drapery I told you about. And remember the color comes from the impurities that have seeped down from the surface.'' She clicked a switch at the box, and the room turned instantly black except for a cluster of spotlights near the top of the cavern placed to show off the colorful deposits on the ceiling. There were panicked squeals from some in the group more than a little uncomfortable at the thought of being deep in a pitch-black cave with no way out. The squeals gave way to gasps of delight as eyes lifted to see the luminous beauty above them.

But two in the group neither saw nor cared to see the calcite drape with its colorful deposits overhead. They kissed again, alone in the blackness of the cavern. In that moment Ellie was as certain as she had ever been of anything in her life that the trip West had changed her life forever. She had found something far more precious than the black gold that had brought her here.

Epilogue

The five friends were enjoying dinner at The Golden Pan. It was a Tuesday in late October, a school night, and they would be leaving for home early. Four of the friends had classes to prepare four, the fifth, Jan, had to hurry home to a new baby, Mark Christopher, born August 18. Erin was to be married Saturday. There would be a bigger party Friday after rehearsal. Tonight's gathering was quiet—five close friends who had shared so much together during college and beyond. They had just raised their wine glasses to the honored guest in heartfelt wishes for her happiness. There was a lull in their cele bration, and Nikki's glance fell on Ellie.

"Ellie, when are you going to take your turn?"

"Go ahead, tell 'em!" Erin practically shouted.

"What?" Alice wanted to know. "Are you next?"

"As a matter of fact . . ." Ellie said with a smile. She had kept her new engagement ring turned diamond in so she wouldn't detract from her roommate's night. Now she slipped it around on her finger and flashed it for all to see. They all craned for a look.

"It's beautiful," said Jan. "When did you get it? Tell us everything."

"Last Saturday night. At The French Café."

"Oh, fancy," Nikki said.

"He gave me a beautiful framed enlargement of Devils Tower where we first met. Well, actually we met before—"

"We've heard that story," Jan broke in. "Get on with the good stuff."

Ellie threw Jan a glare, but she didn't really mean it. "Well, he had taped the ring at the top of the Tower, right on the glass of the frame so it looked like a star on a Christmas tree."

"How romantic," Nikki gushed.

"It would have been better if I hadn't spoiled it," Ellie had to admit. "I didn't even see it. He finally had to show it to me before I put it back in the wrapping."

"So, he said, 'No way am I going to marry someone that stupid,' " Erin chimed in, "and he called it off."

"Very funny," Ellie said, with a grin at her roommate, "but I kept the diamond." She held up her hand.

"That's not true, is it?" Nikki wailed.

"That I kept the diamond? Sure."

"You know what I mean."

"Nope. We're getting married June sixteenth, and you're all in the wedding party."

"I should hope so," Alice said. "So are you going to travel with him all over the world?"

"That's my second piece of news. Remember I told you about the B-and-B travel book he wants to do?" They all nodded. "Well, a publisher picked it up, gave him a nice advance and everything. We're going to travel the first four months gathering material for the book."

"That sounds so exciting." It was Nikki again.

"And after that he's going to settle into an editor's job if it's available, which he thinks it will be."

"That means you're going to be moving away." The friends were all thinking it, but Nikki had put it into words.

"Just to Chicago," Erin informed them, "and that must not be too far away 'cause he comes here or she goes there every weekend."

"Not every weekend."

"Just about."

"What about his family?" asked Jan.

"That's my third piece of news. Graham found his uncle just last week."

There was a chorus of exclamations at that news. They had all heard of the missing uncle.

"He's a retired accountant who lives in San Diego. He's coming to visit them this weekend, and Graham's mother is just about out of control."

"Don't forget to tell them about Lil," Erin prompted.

"You mean the woman at the motel?" Jan asked. "The one who got you two together?"

"Right. We called her to tell her about the engagement, and she promised to come to the wedding, so you'll all get to meet her. You're going to love her."

"This all sounds like something you'd see on one of those talk shows," Alice said. "Now, if you got your hands on some oil, you'd have a real story."

"We're working on it. It isn't out of the realm of possibility."

"You're kidding!"

"We're trying to see if we can prove Whitiker gained Graham's grandfather's oil rights fraudulently. If we can, he and his mother would be able to make a claim on the company that bought out Whitiker and so would my mom and I."

"That would be something," Jan said with a smile and a shake of the head.

"As I remember, a certain somebody in this little group said I was going on a wild goose chase," Ellie said, her eye on her friend Jan. "And whoever said that couldn't have been more wrong."